D0604151

A PLUME BOOK

T-REX TRYING AND TRYING

DR. HUGH MURPHY graduated from dental school at the
University of Southern California and is currently in his
residency at UNC Chapel Hill for advanced prostho-
dontics. He loves drawing, painting, fly-fishing, nature
programs, and most of all, his wife, Sarah.

T-REX TRYING
AND TRYING...

The unfortunate trials of a
modern prehistoric family.

Hugh Murphy

A PLUME BOOK

PLUME
Penguin Group (USA) LLC
375 Hudson Street
New York, New York 10014

USA | Canada | UK | Ireland | Australia | New Zealand | India | South Africa | China
penguin.com
A Penguin Random House Company

First published by Plume, a member of Penguin Group (USA) LLC, 2014

Some illustrations previously appeared on the author's blog, http://trextrying.tumblr.com

REGISTERED TRADEMARK—MARCA REGISTRADA

ISBN 978-0-14-218170-6

Printed in the United States of America
10 9 8 7 6 5 4 3 2 1

Set in Ego Com Regular

For my family, the greatest source of inspiration, joy, and love in my life

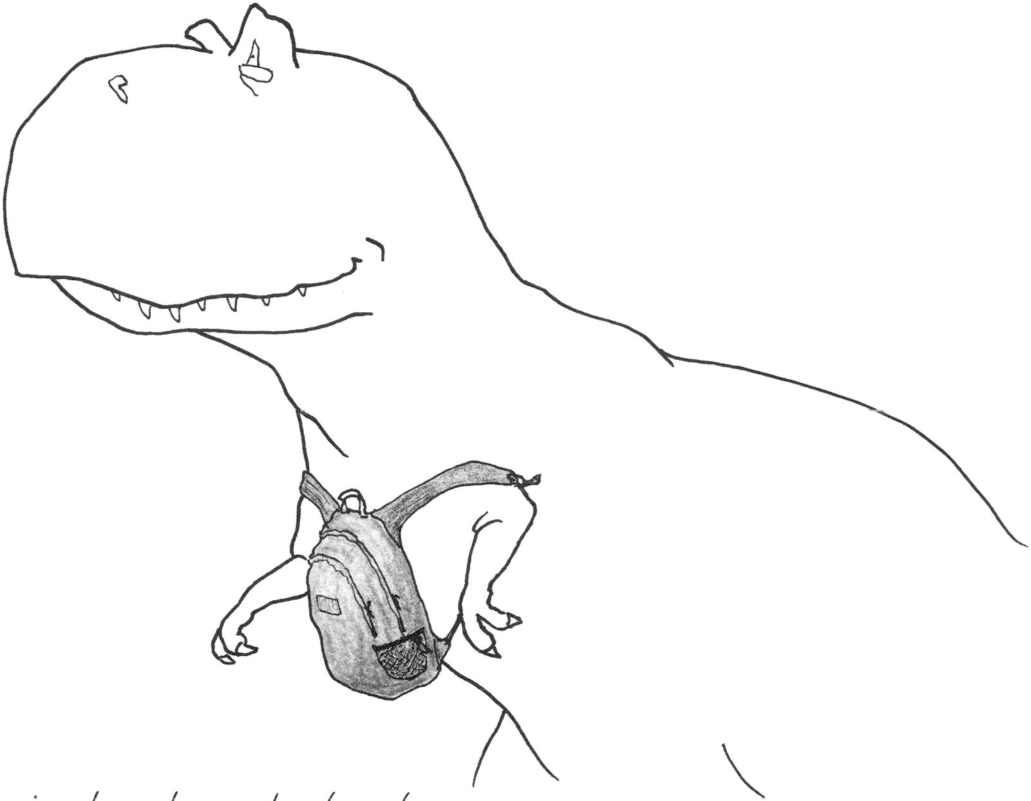

T-Rex trying to put on a backpack . . .

T-Rex trying to reach his fanny pack . . .

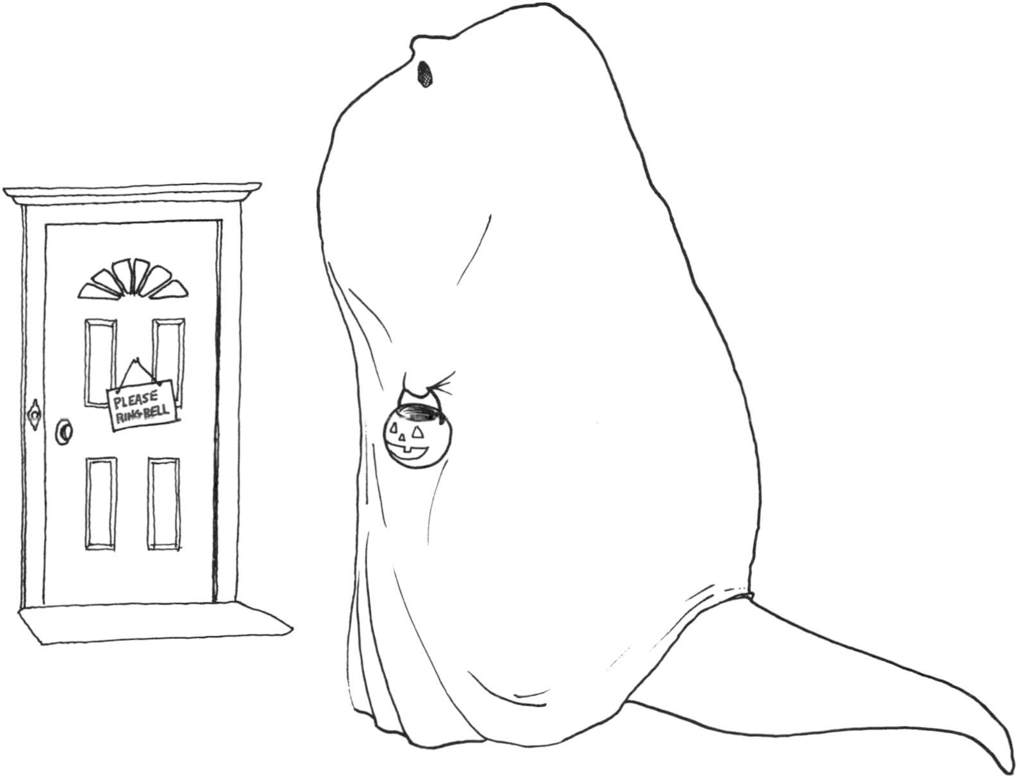
PLEASE
RING BELL

T-Rex trying to go trick-or-treating . . .

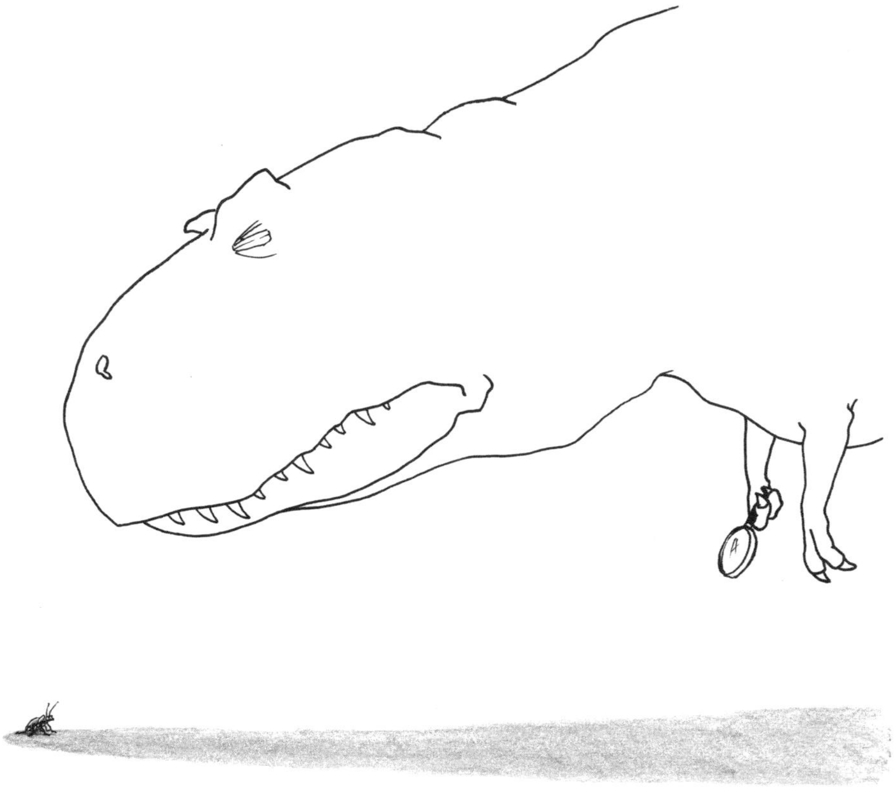

T-Rex trying to use a magnifying glass . . .

T-Rex trying to use a pogo stick . . .

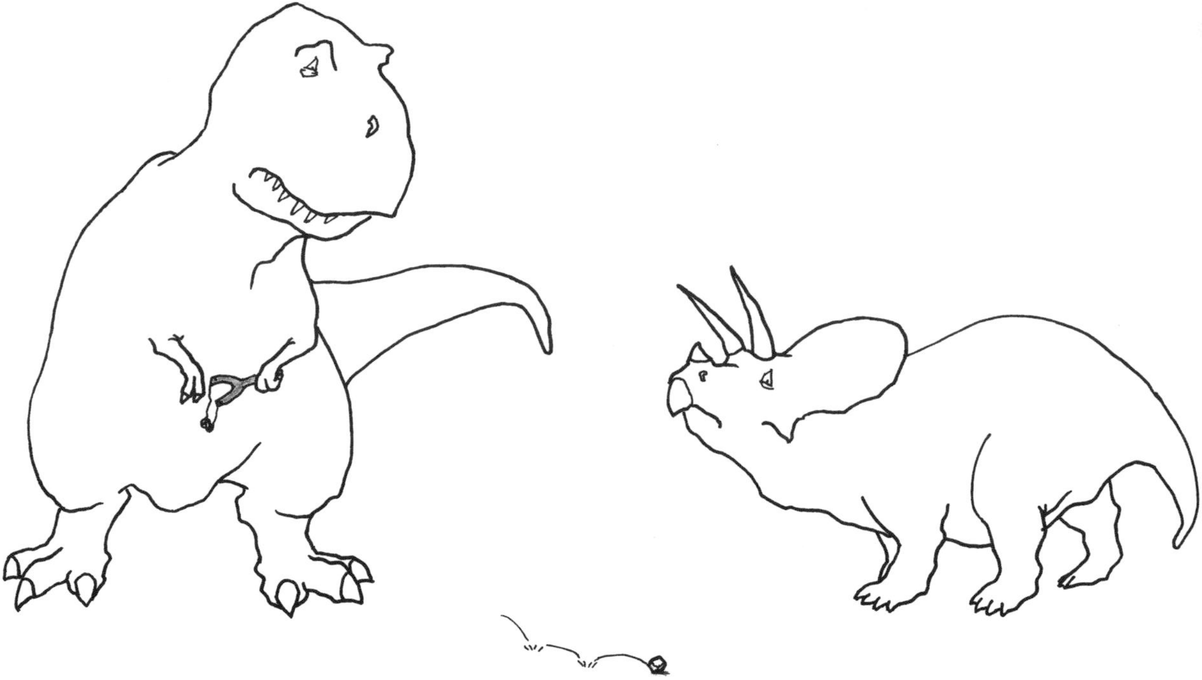

T-Rex trying to use a slingshot . . .

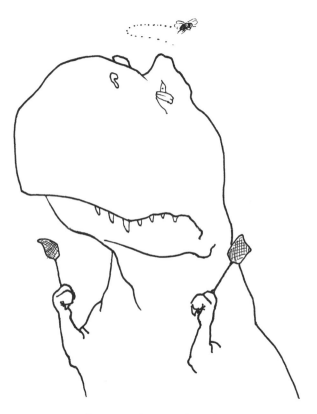

T-Rex trying to hurt a fly . . .

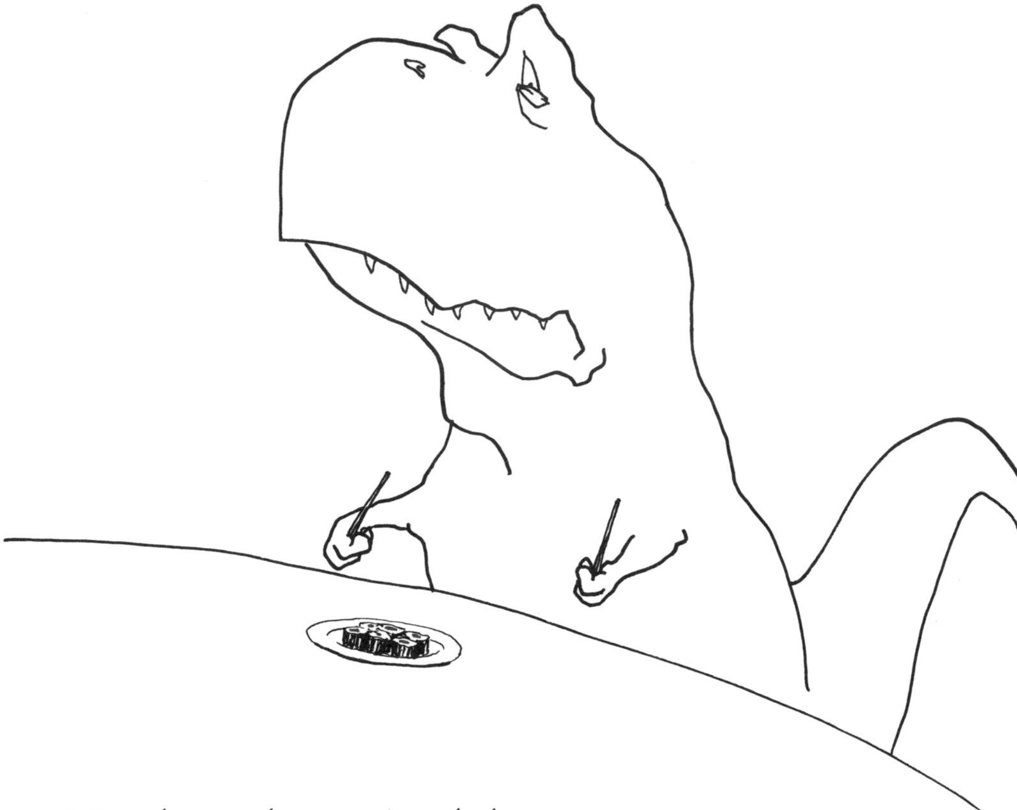

T-Rex trying to use chopsticks . . .

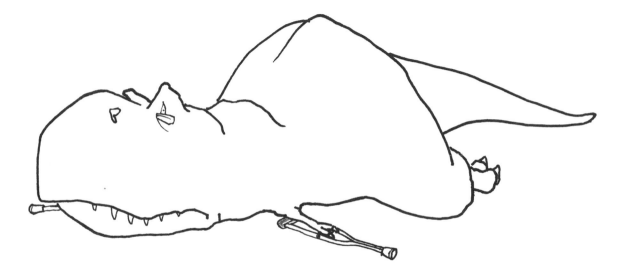

T-Rex trying to use crutches . . .

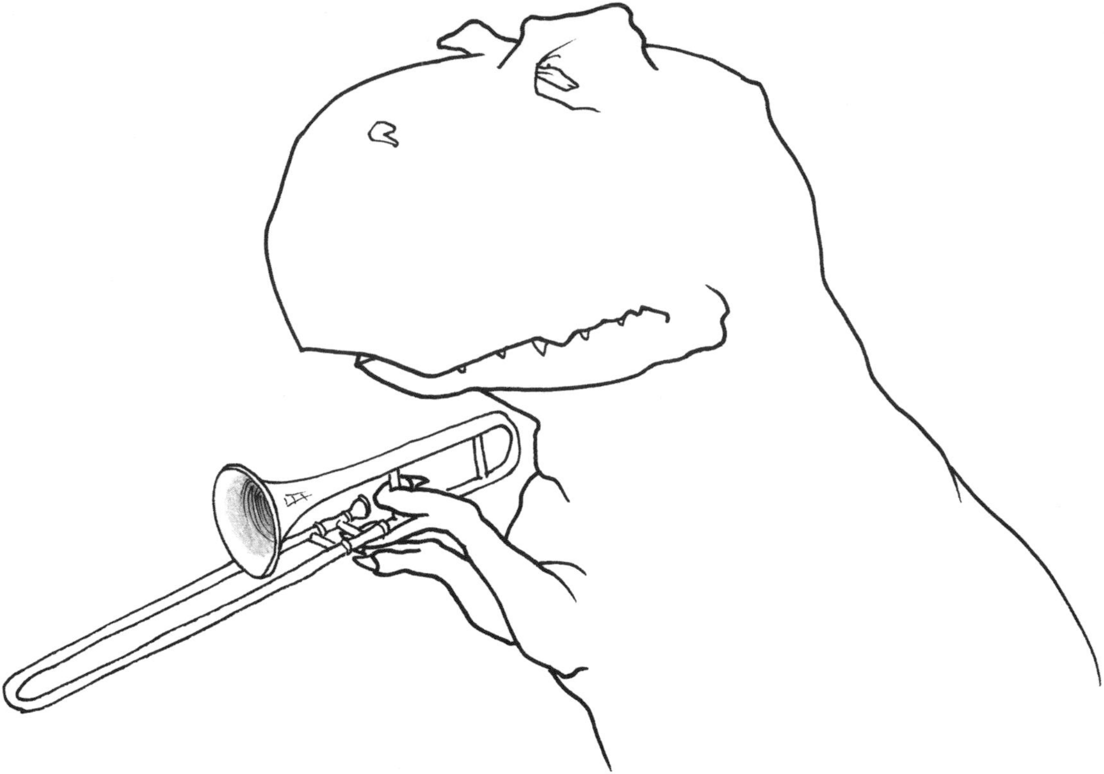

T-Rex trying to play the trombone . . .

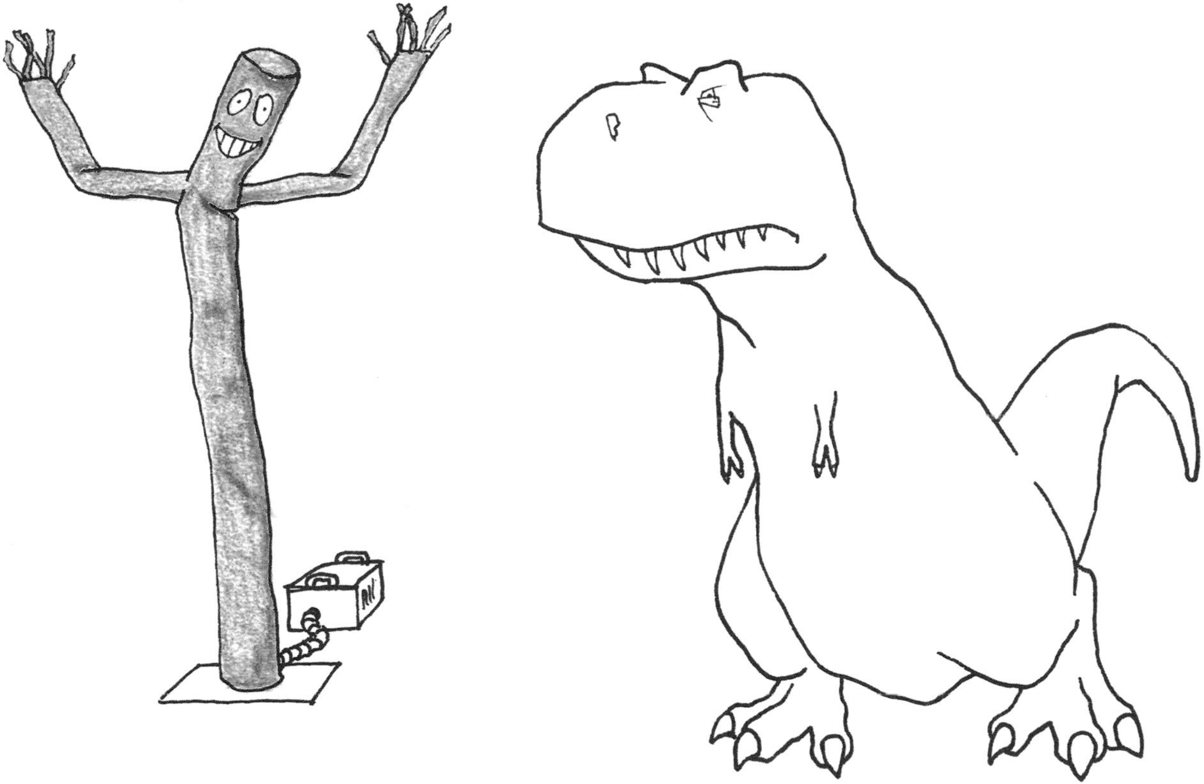

T-Rex trying to control his jealousy . . .

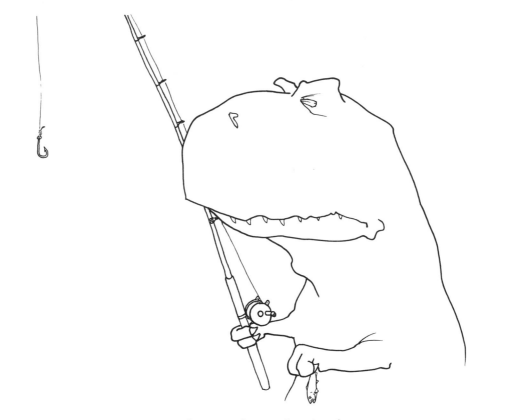

T-Rex trying to bait a hook . . .

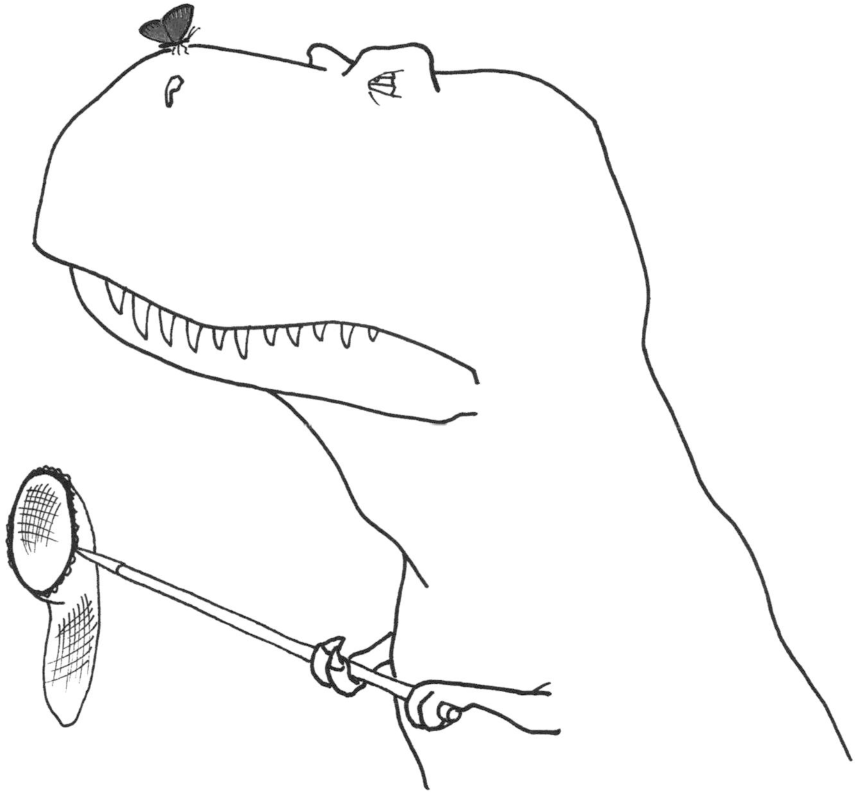

T-Rex trying to catch a butterfly . . .

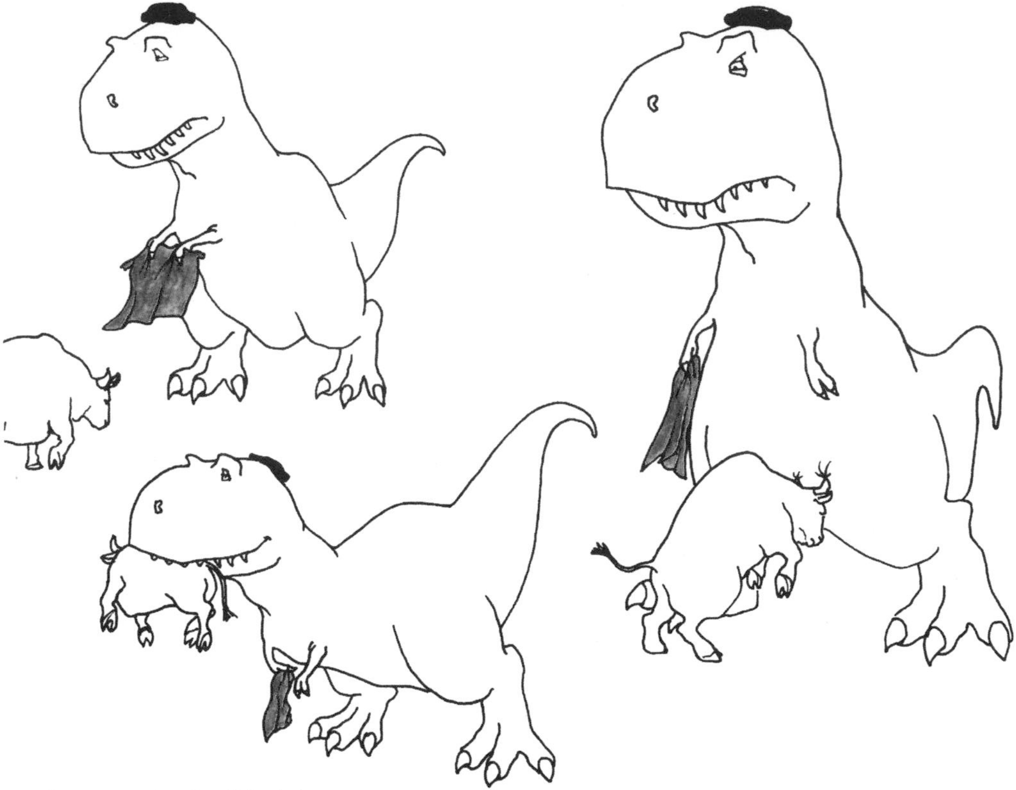

T-Rex trying to bullfight . . .

T-Rex trying to blow a whistle . . .

T-Rex trying to surrender from a trench . . .

T-Rex trying to catch a fly ball . . .

T-Rex trying to catch another fly ball . . .

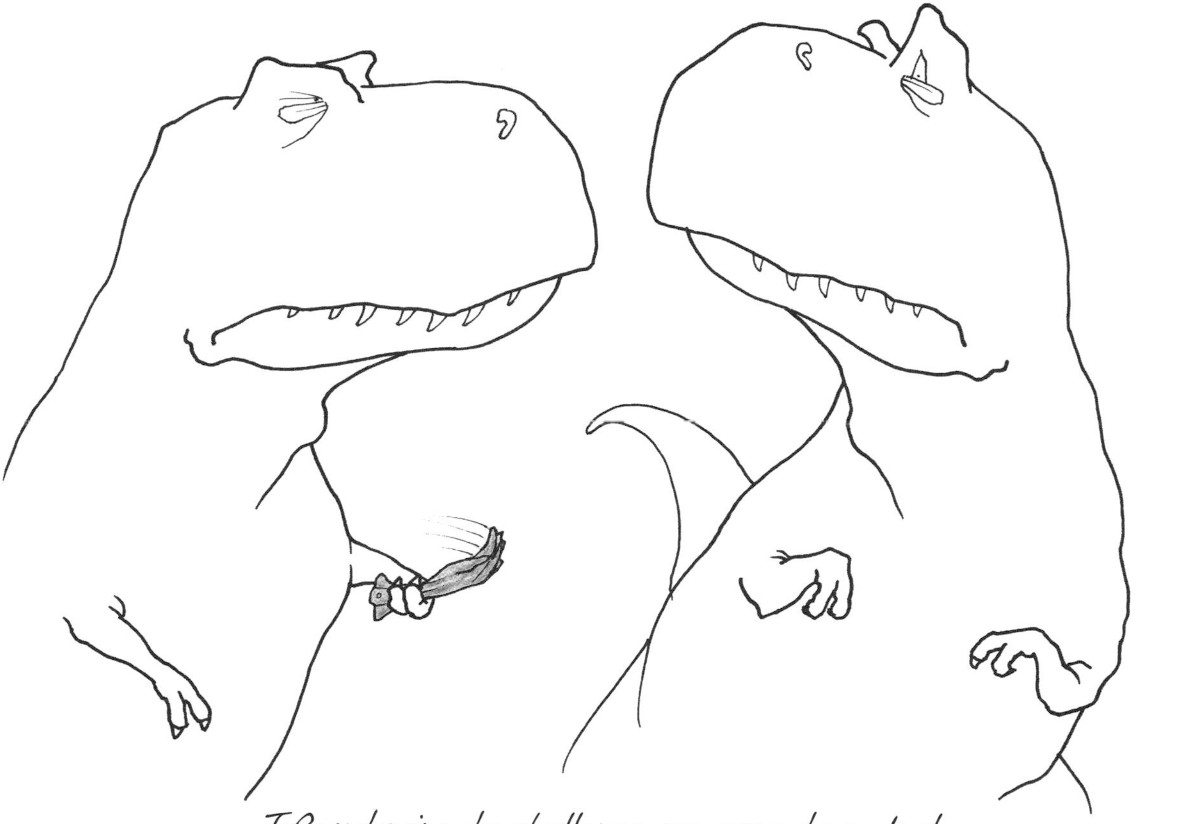

T-Rex trying to challenge someone to a duel . . .

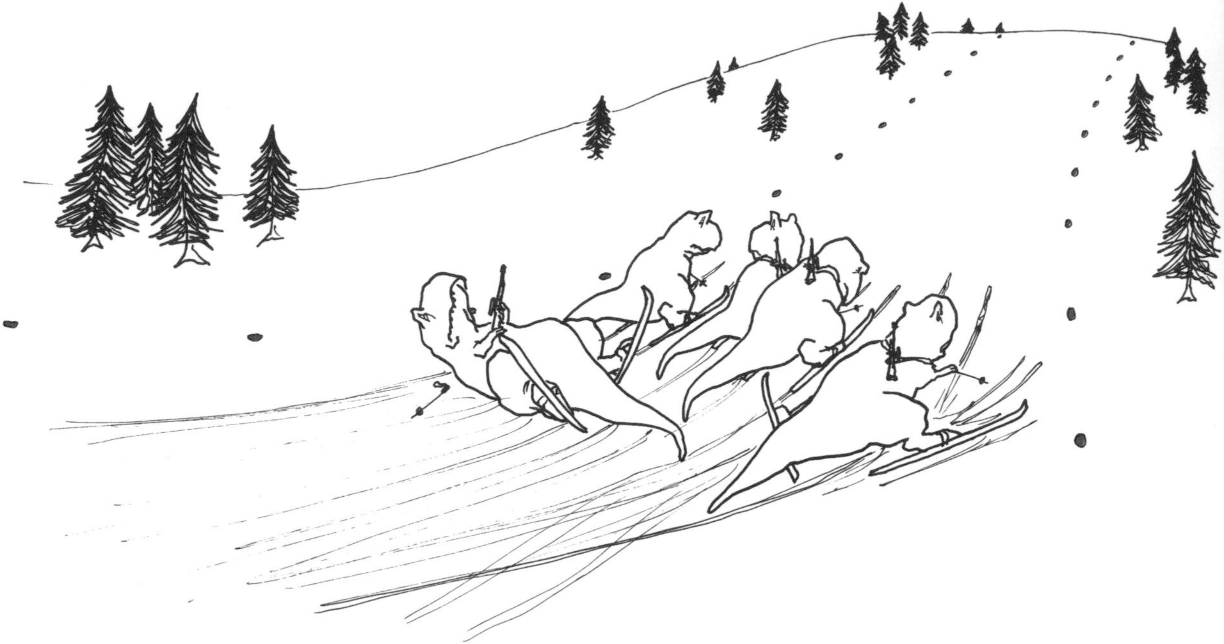

T-Rexes trying the biathlon . . .

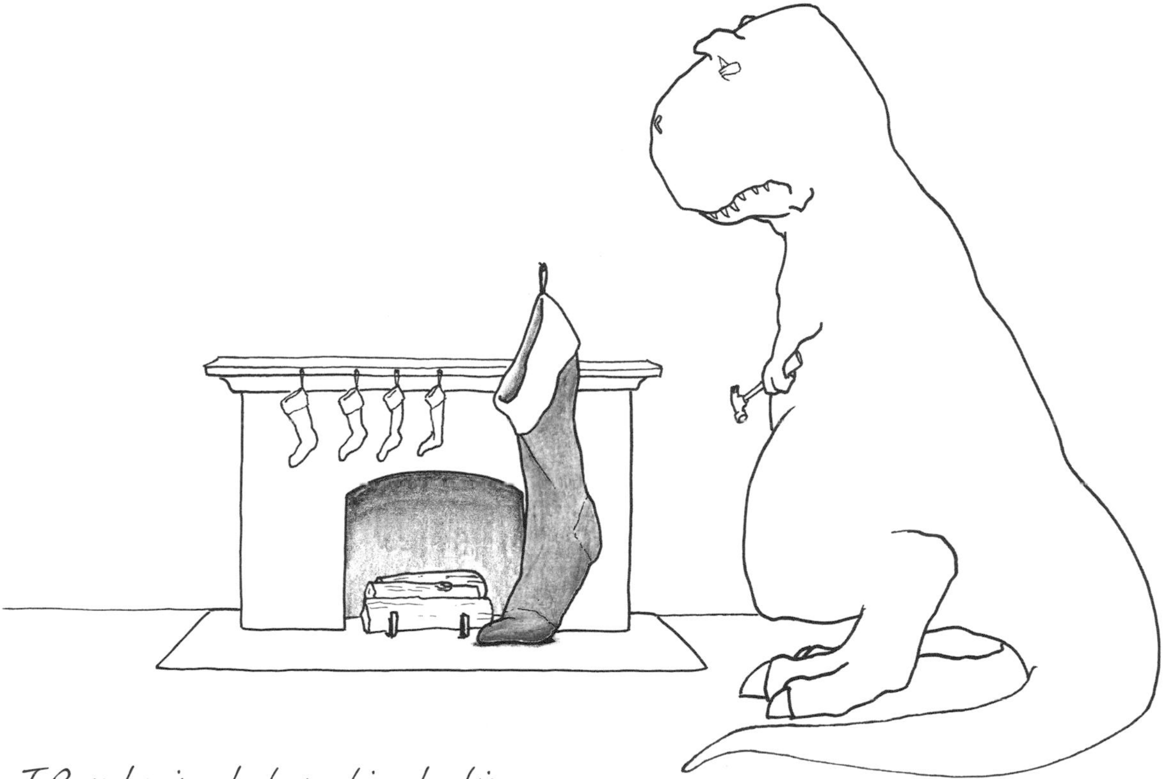

T-Rex trying to hang his stocking . . .

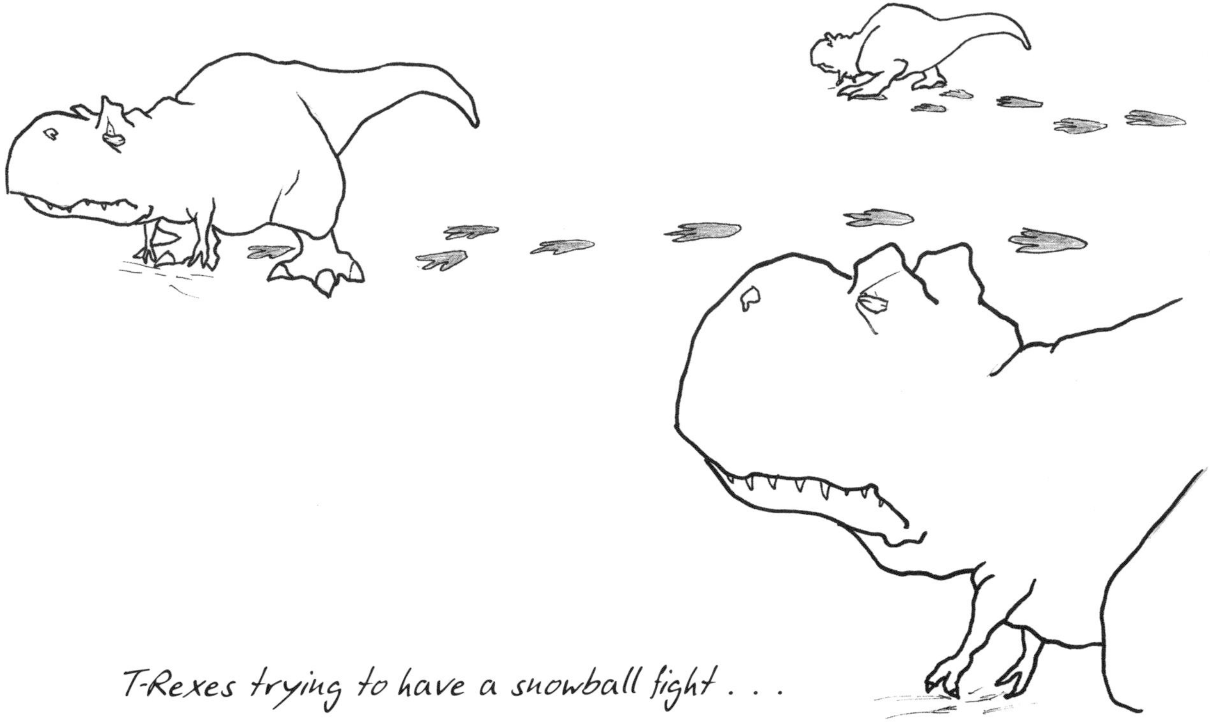

T-Rexes trying to have a snowball fight . . .

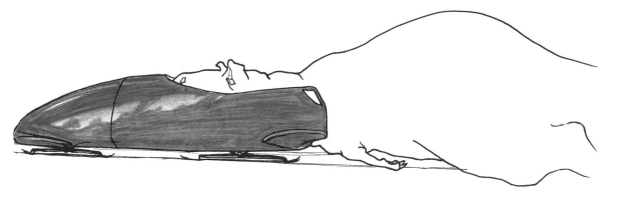

T-Rex trying to bobsled . . .

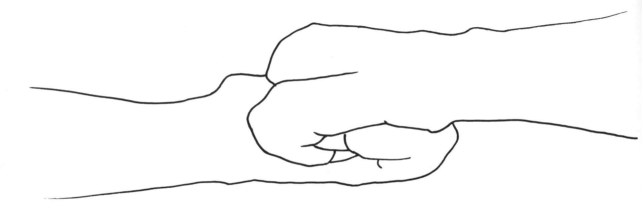

T-Rexes trying to thumb wrestle . . .

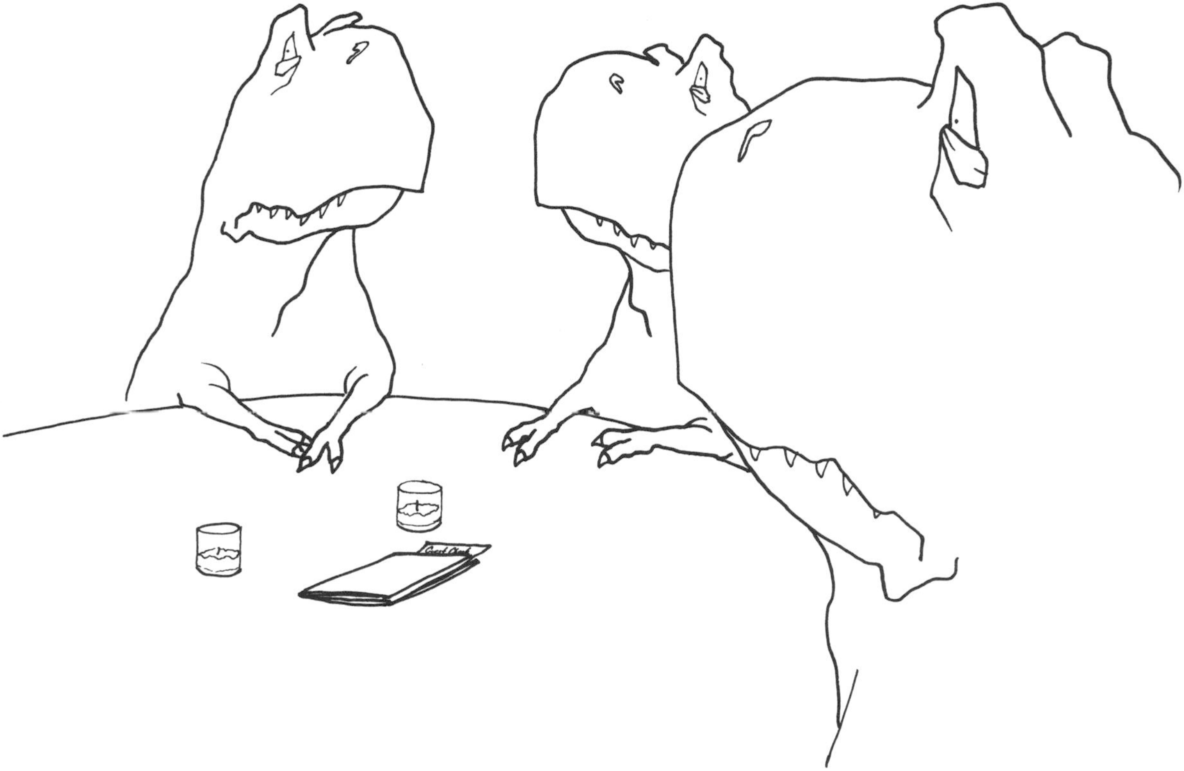

T-Rexes trying to pay the check . . .

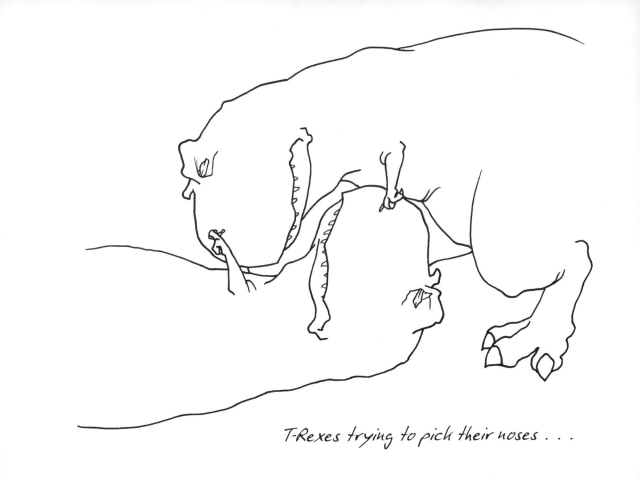

T-Rexes trying to pick their noses . . .

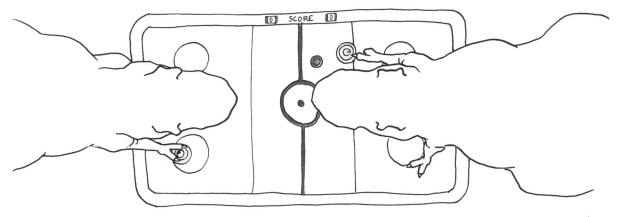

T-Rexes trying to play air hockey . . .

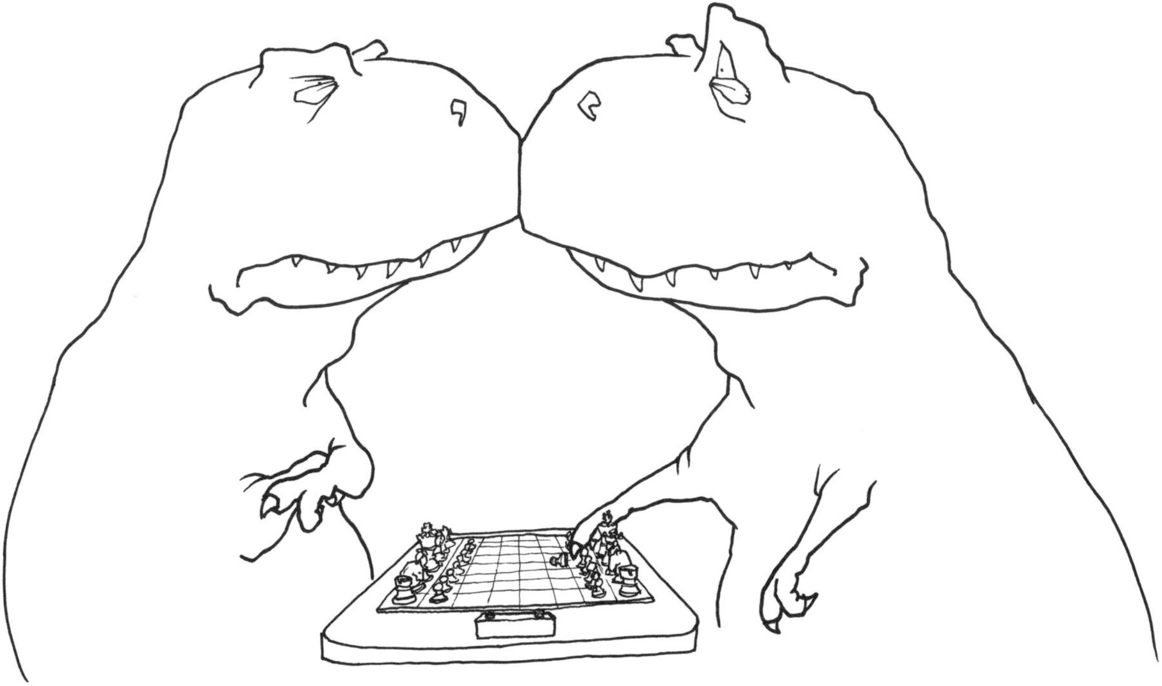

T-Rexes trying to play chess . . .

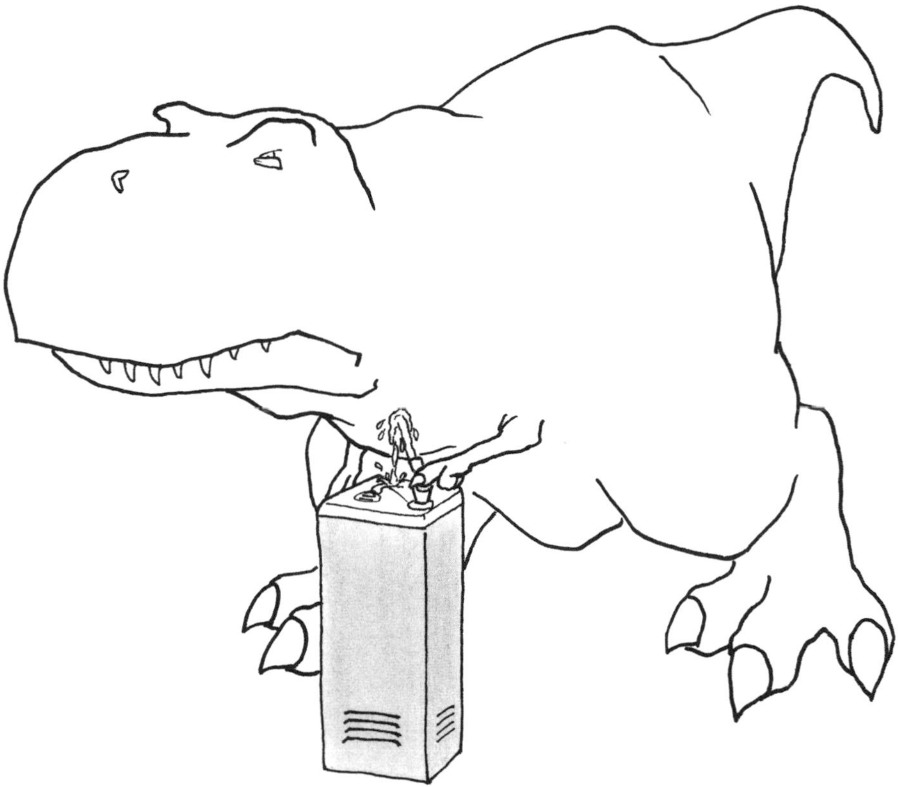

T-Rex trying to drink from a water fountain . . .

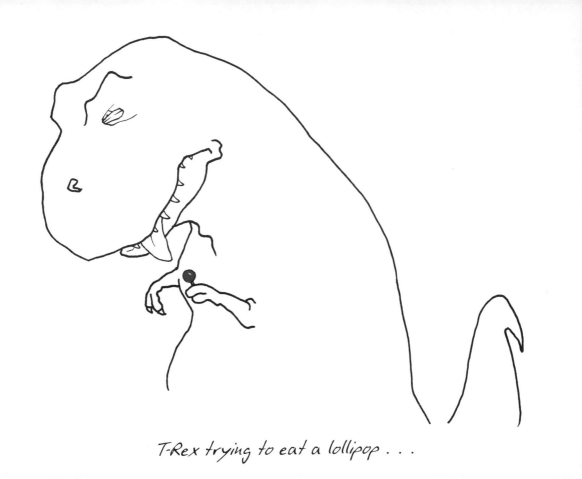

T-Rex trying to eat a lollipop . . .

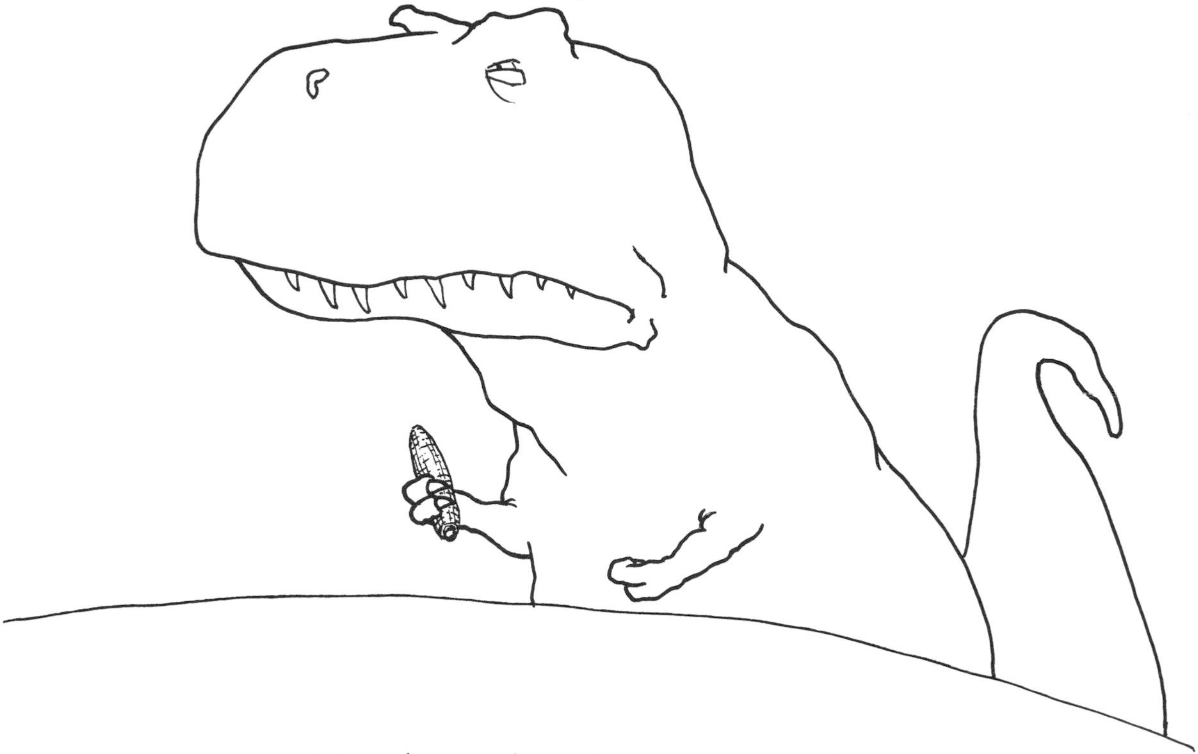

T-Rex trying to eat corn on the cob . . .

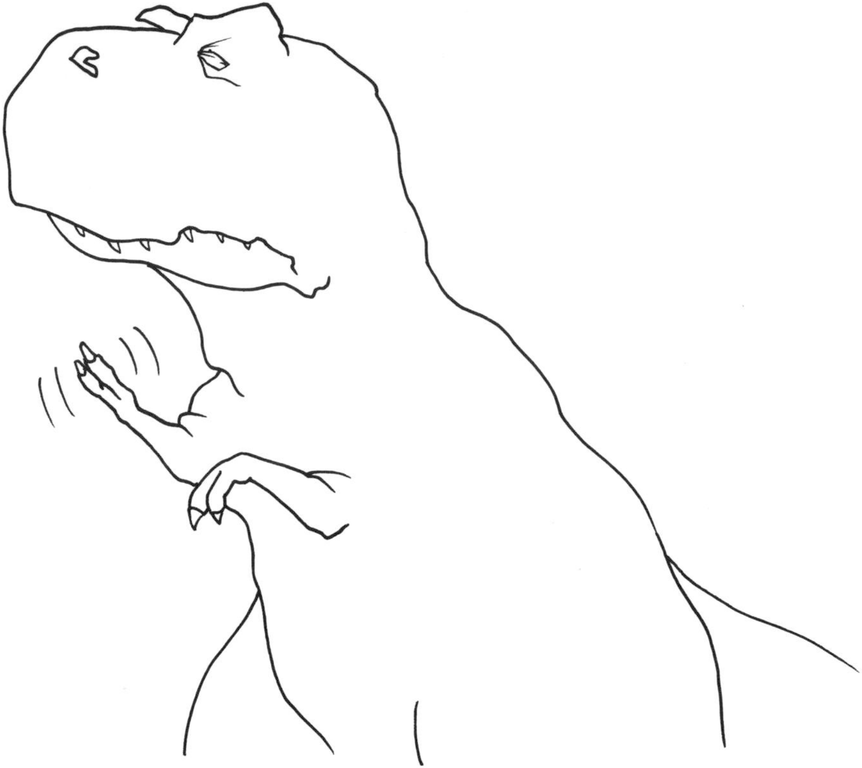

T-Rex trying to fan away a fart . . .

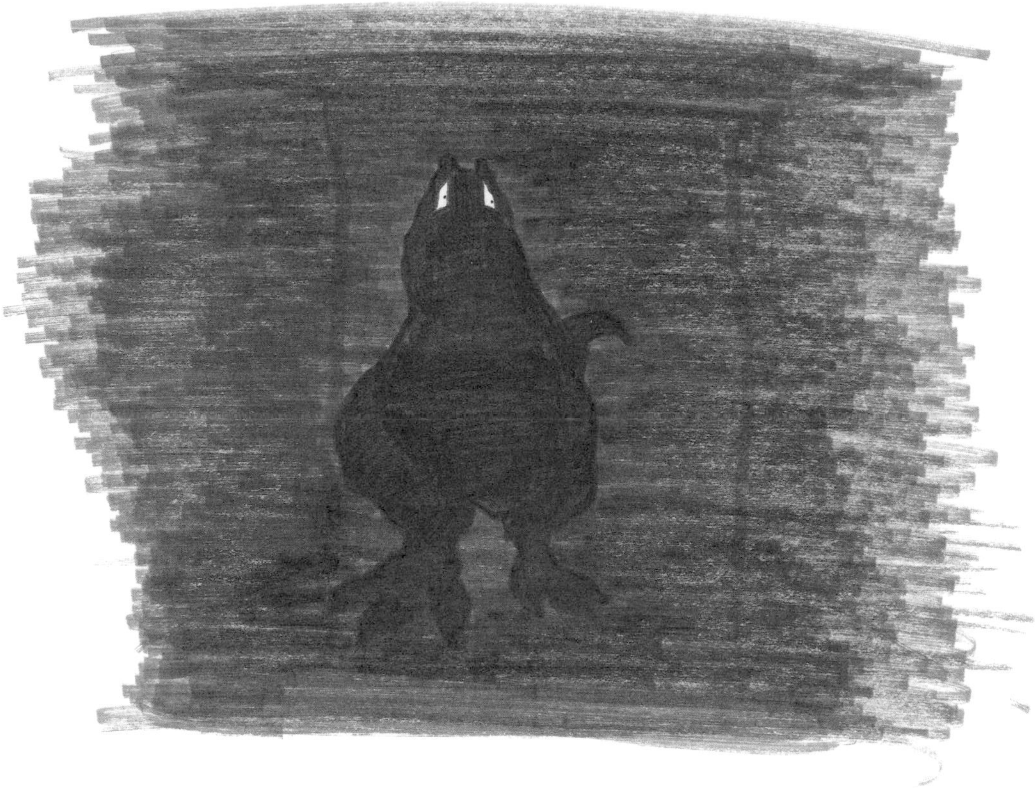

T-Rex trying to find the light switch . . .

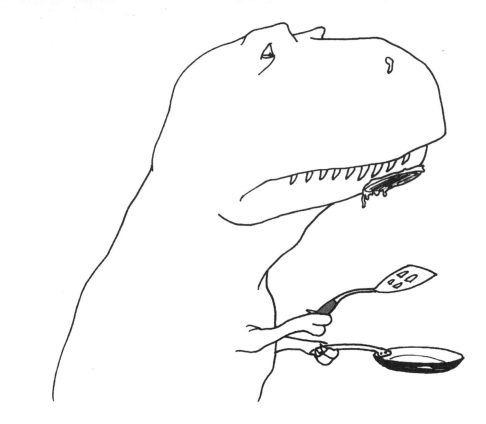

T-Rex trying to flip a pancake . . .

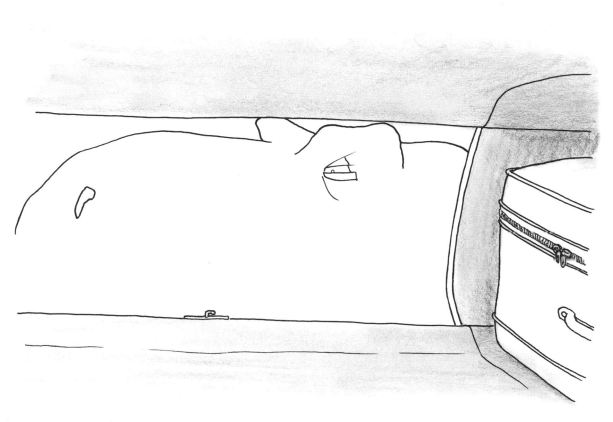

T-Rex trying to stow his bag in the overhead compartment . . .

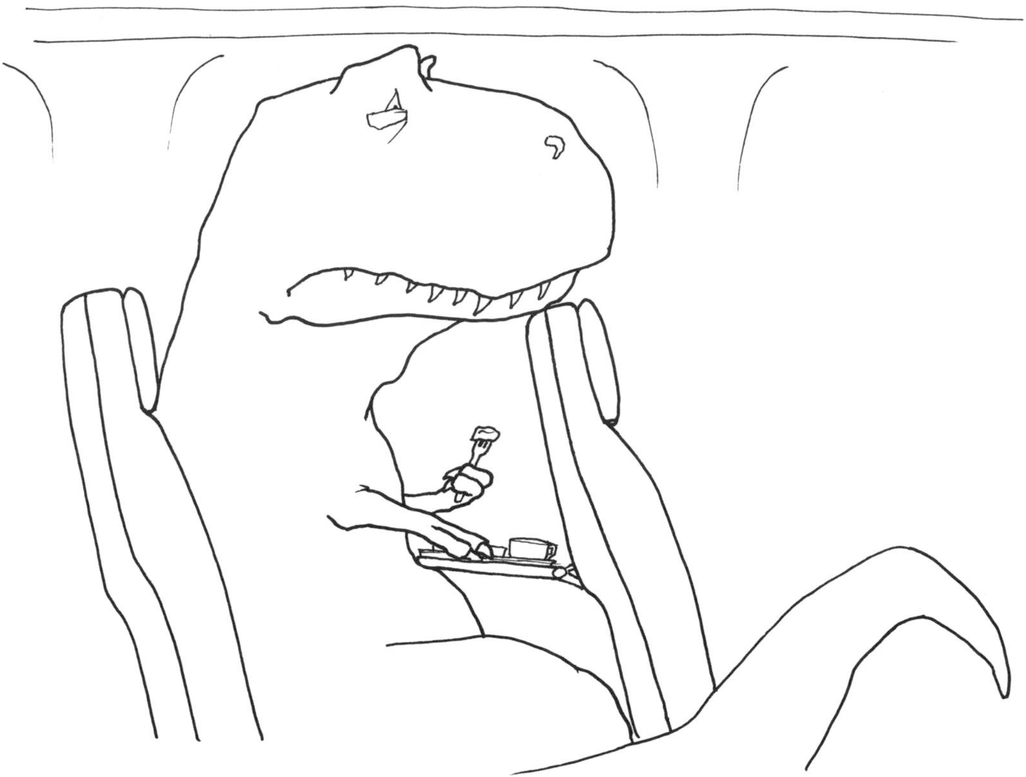

T-Rex trying to eat dinner on an international flight . . .

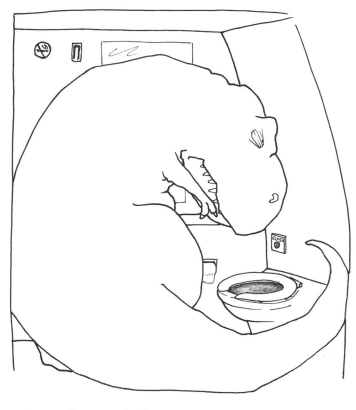

T-Rex trying to flush an airplane toilet . . .

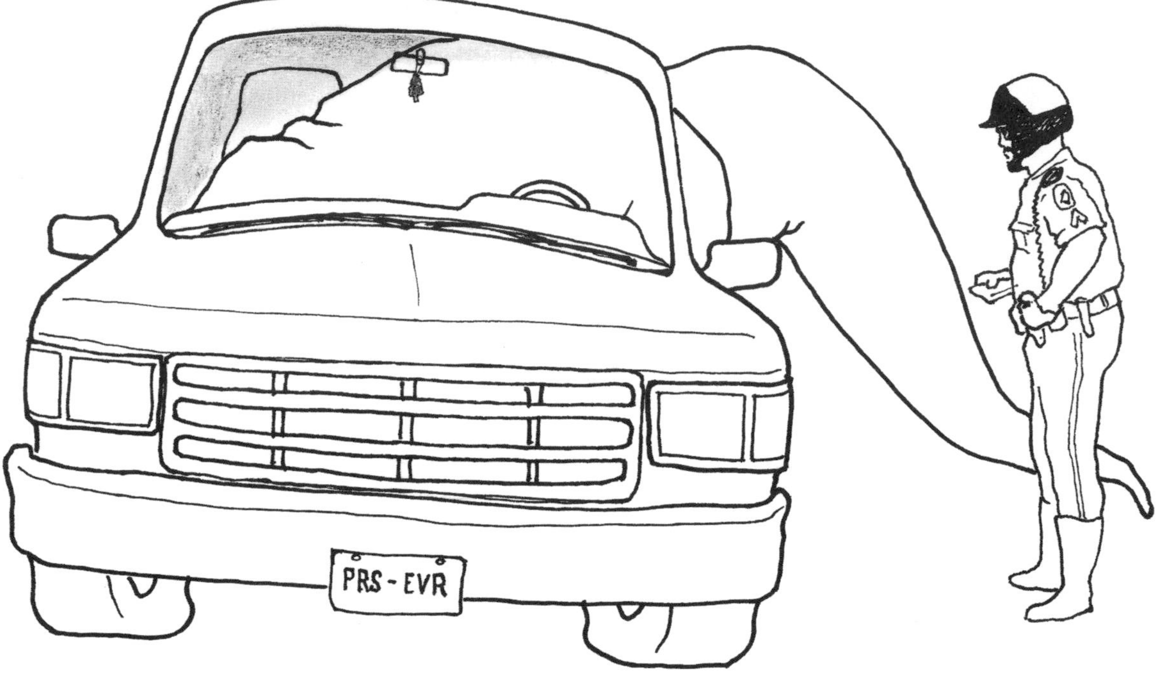
PRS - EVR

T-Rex trying to get his license and registration . . .

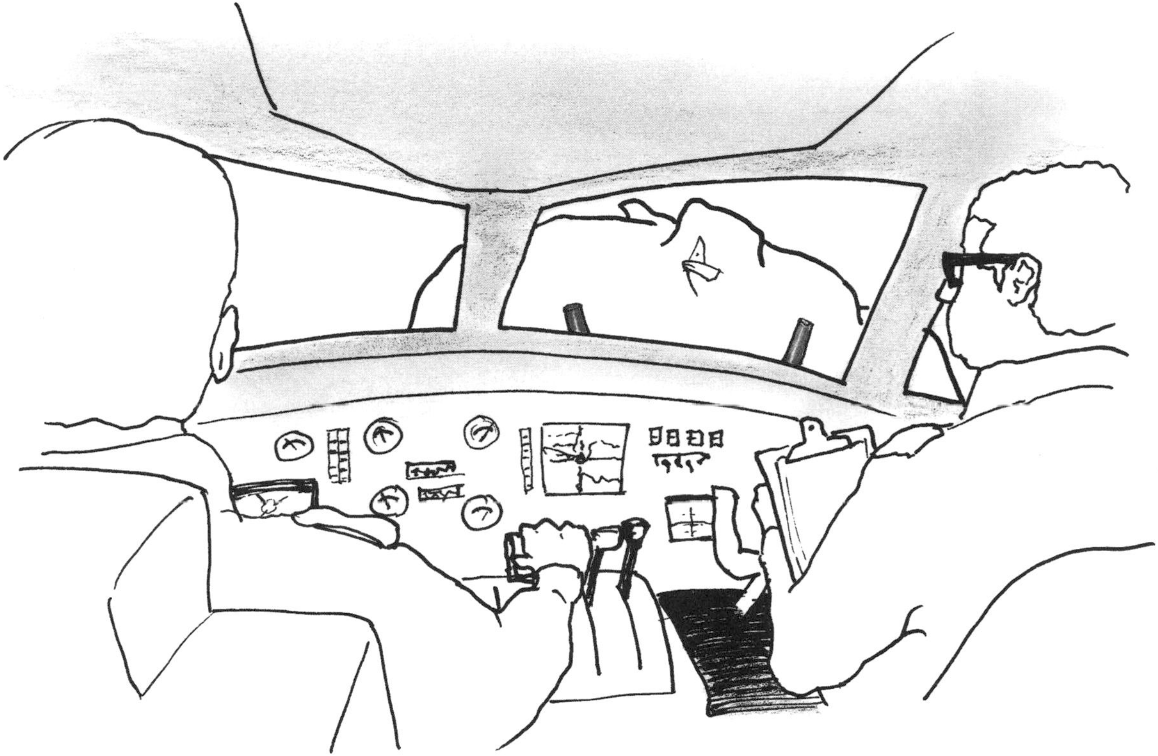

T-Rex trying to guide a plane to its gate . . .

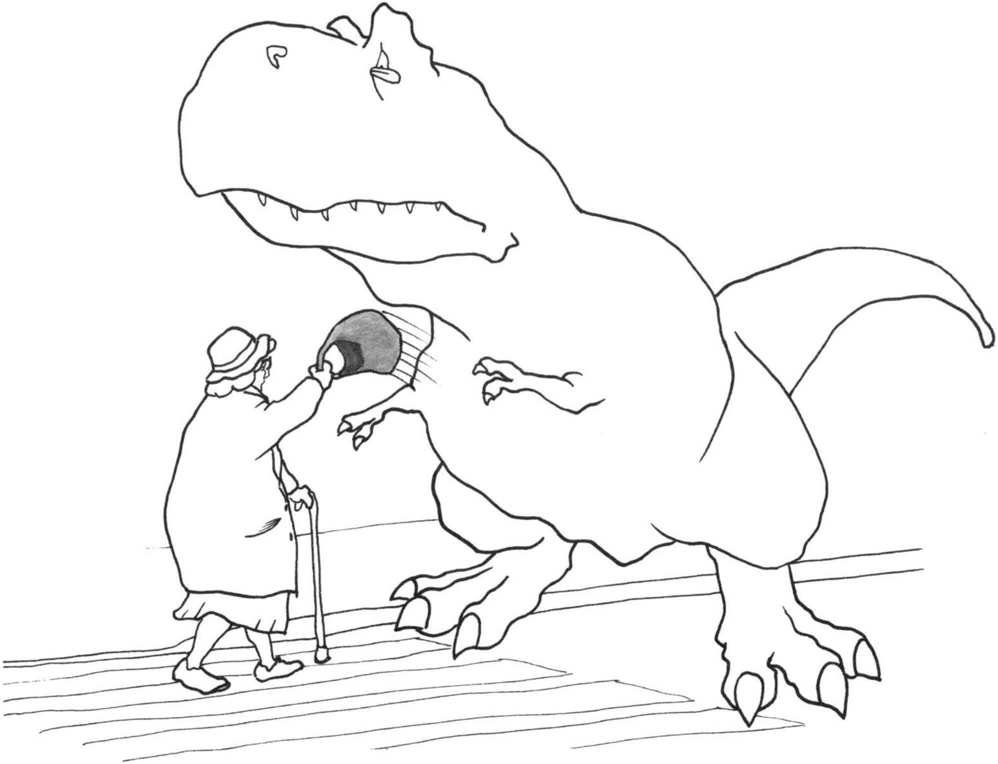

T-Rex trying to help an old lady cross the street . . .

T-Rex trying to toot his own horn . . .

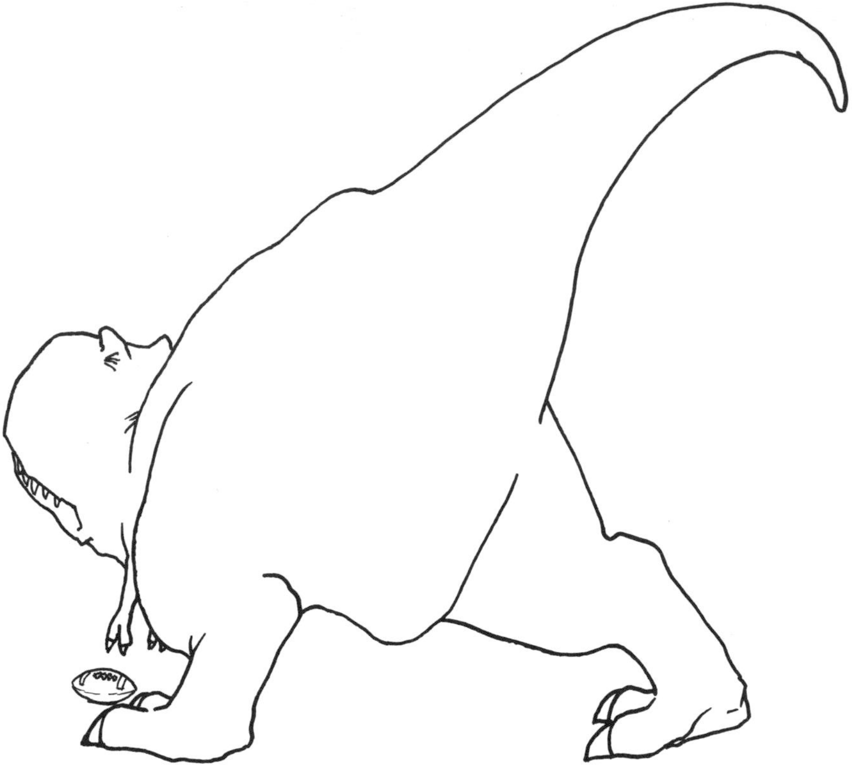

T-Rex trying to hike a football . . .

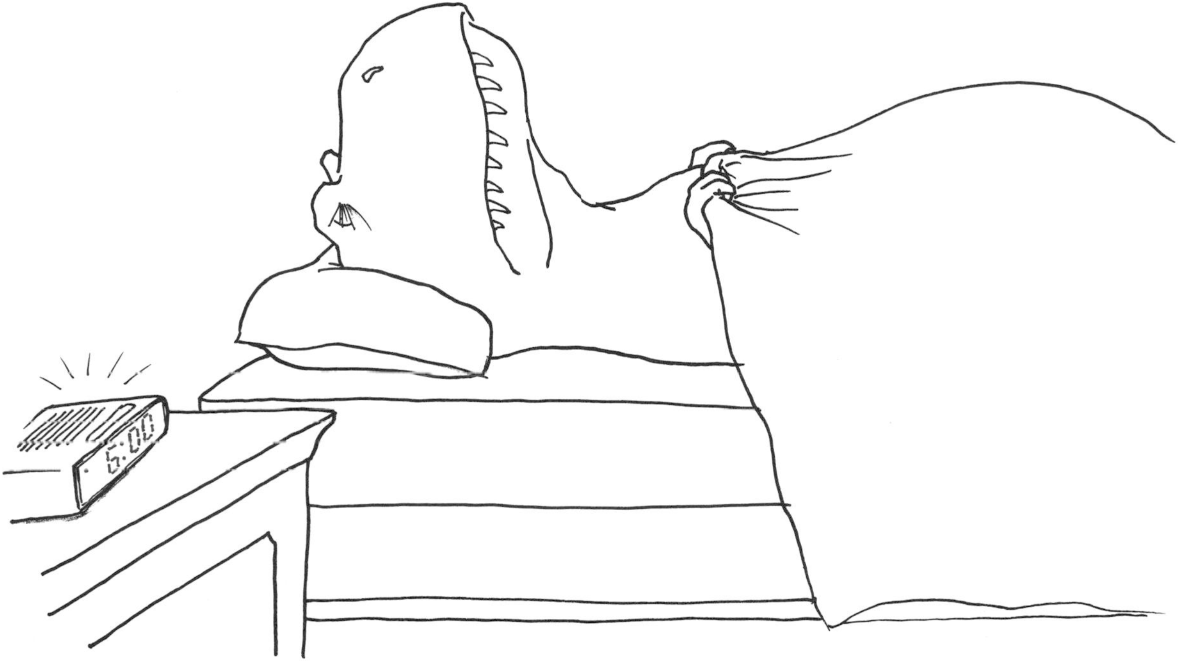
5:00

T-Rex trying to hit the snooze button . . .

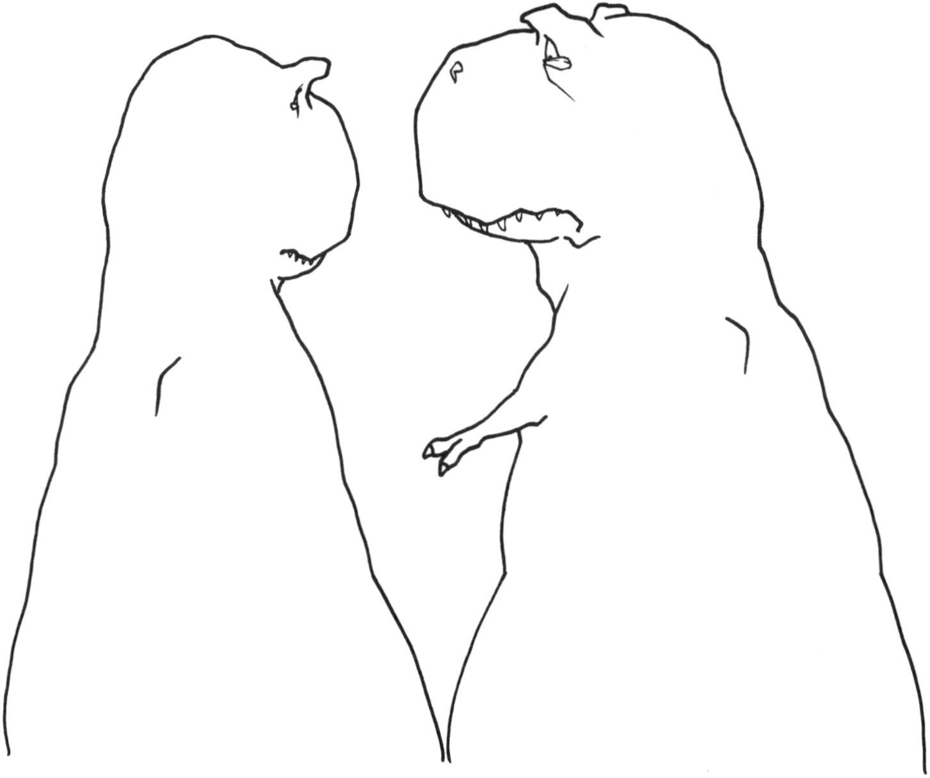

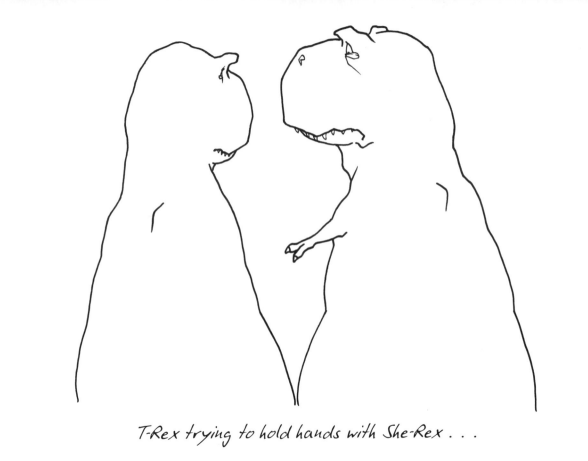

T-Rex trying to hold hands with She-Rex . . .

T-Rex trying to use a Hula-Hoop . . .

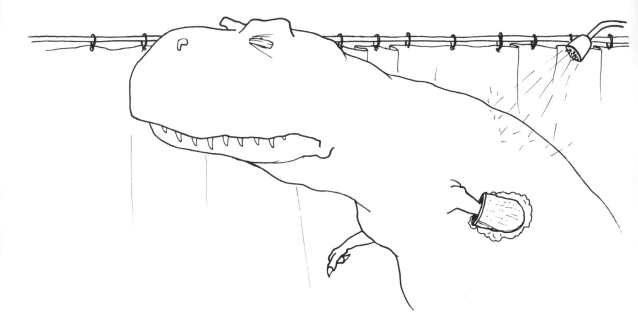

T-Rex trying to loofah his back . . .

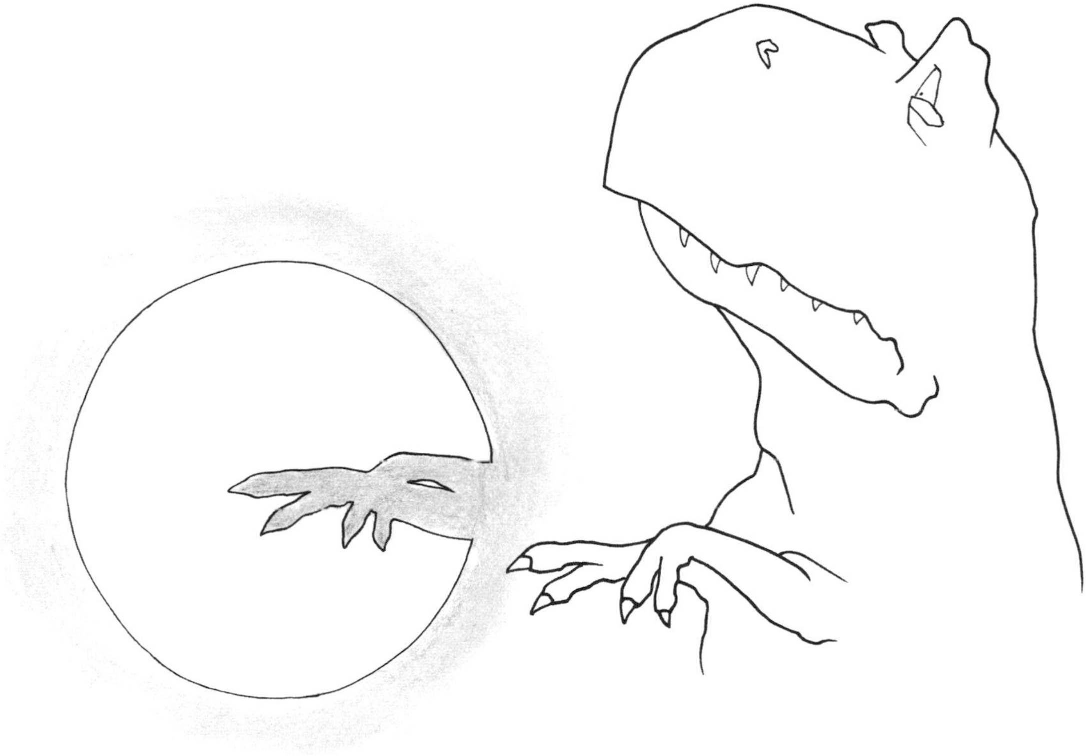

T-Rex trying to make shadow puppets . . .

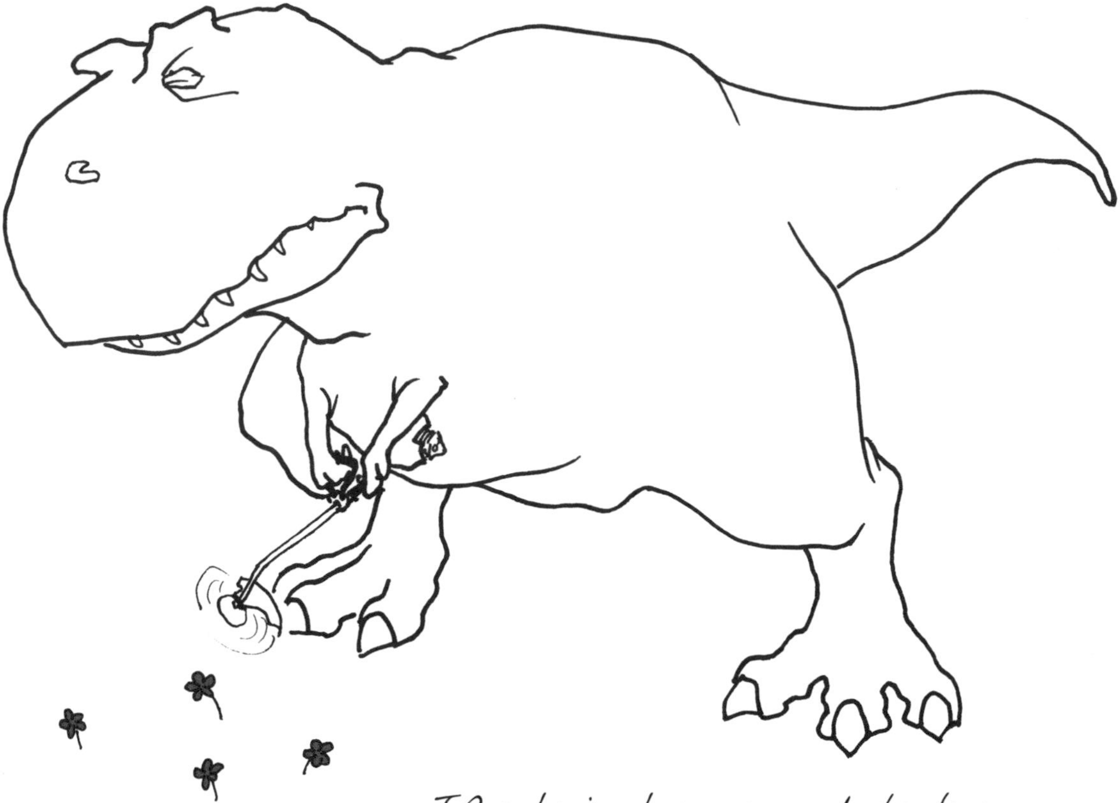

T-Rex trying to use a weed whacker . . .

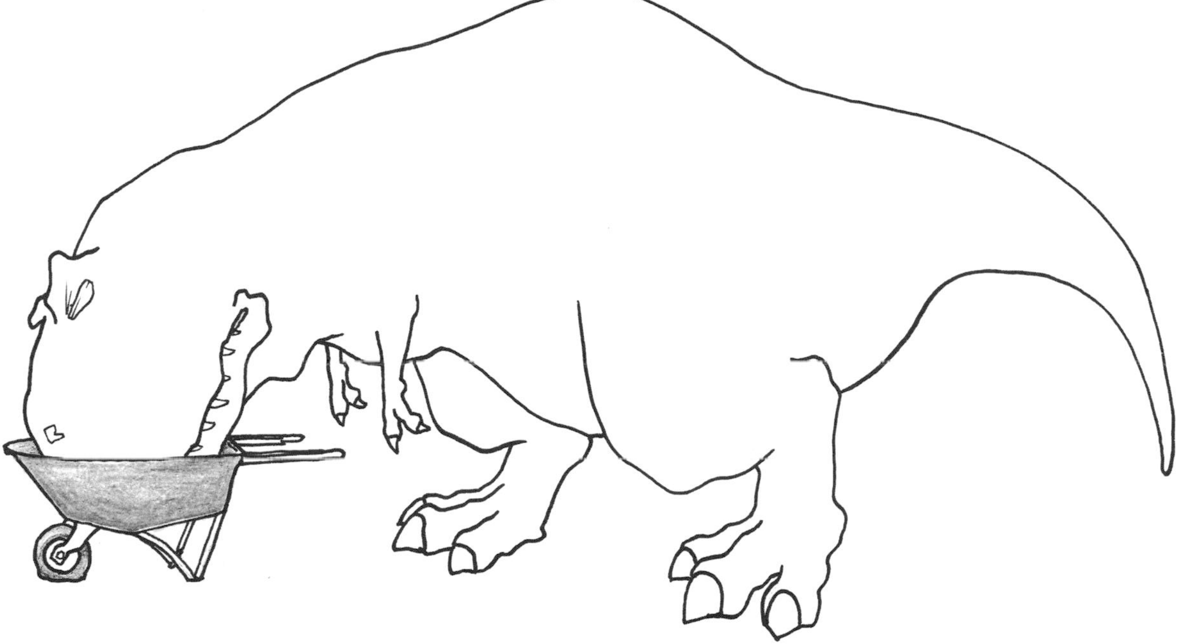

T-Rex trying to use a wheelbarrow . . .

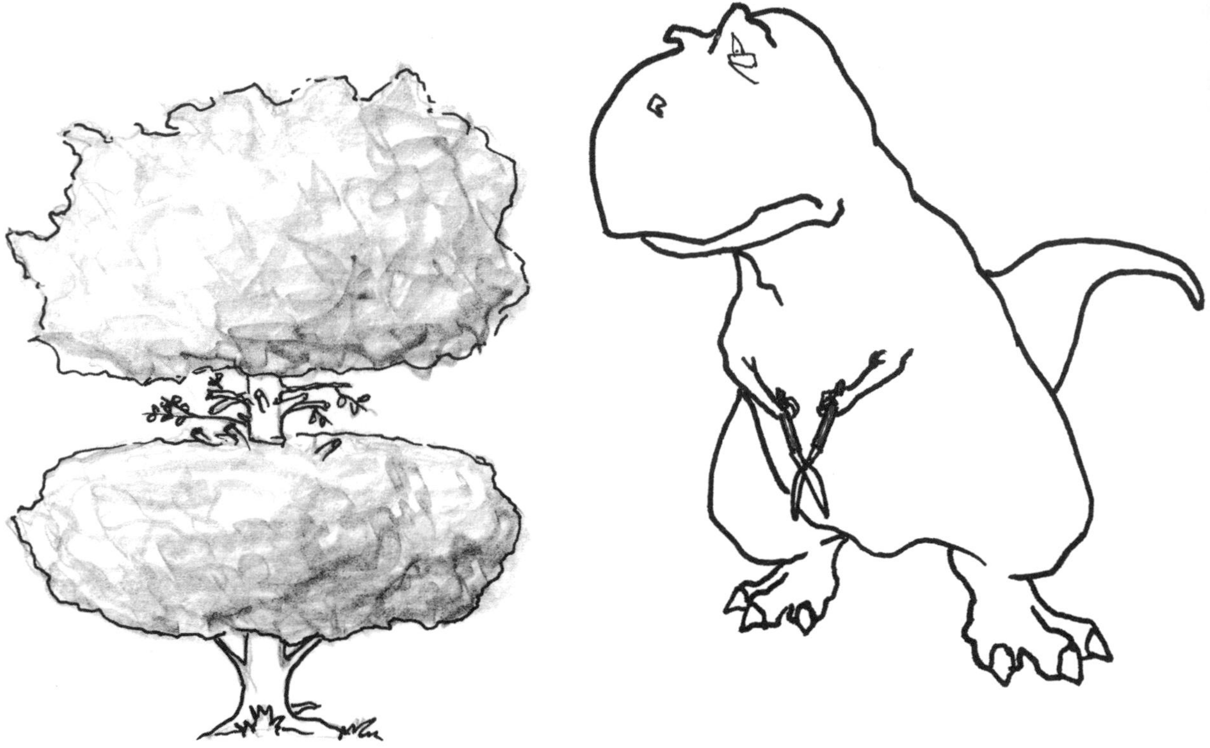

T-Rex trying to landscape . . .

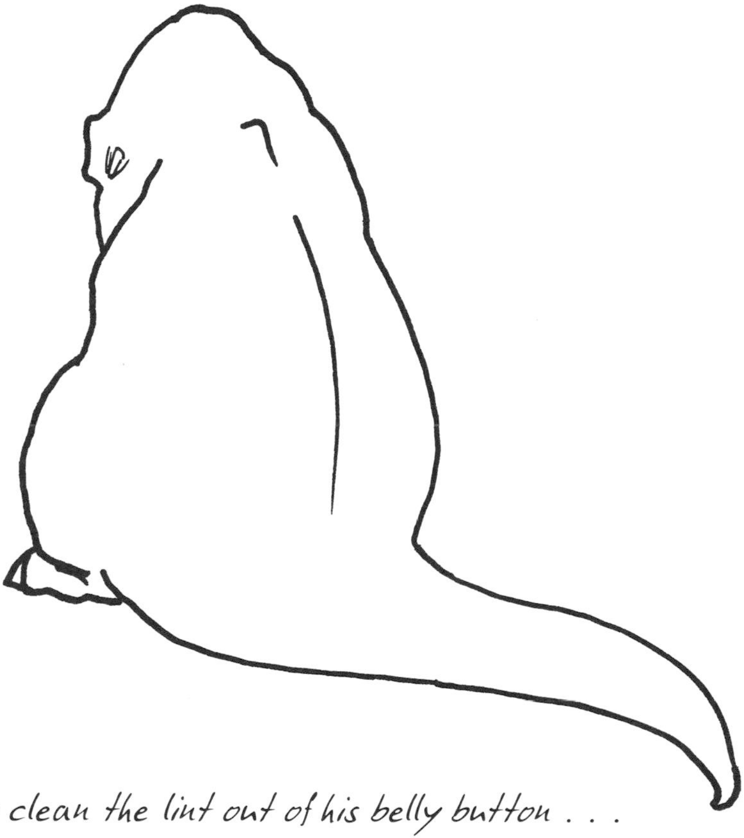

T-Rex trying to clean the lint out of his belly button . . .

T-Rex trying to measure his inseam . . .

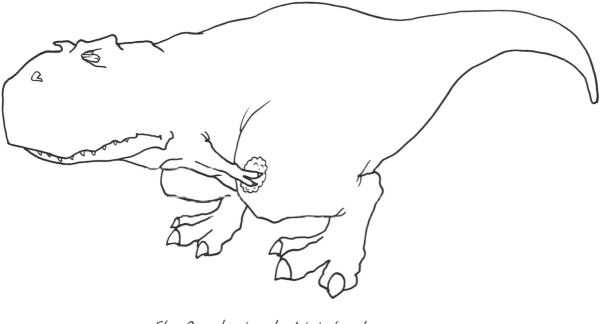

She-Rex trying to Nair her legs . . .

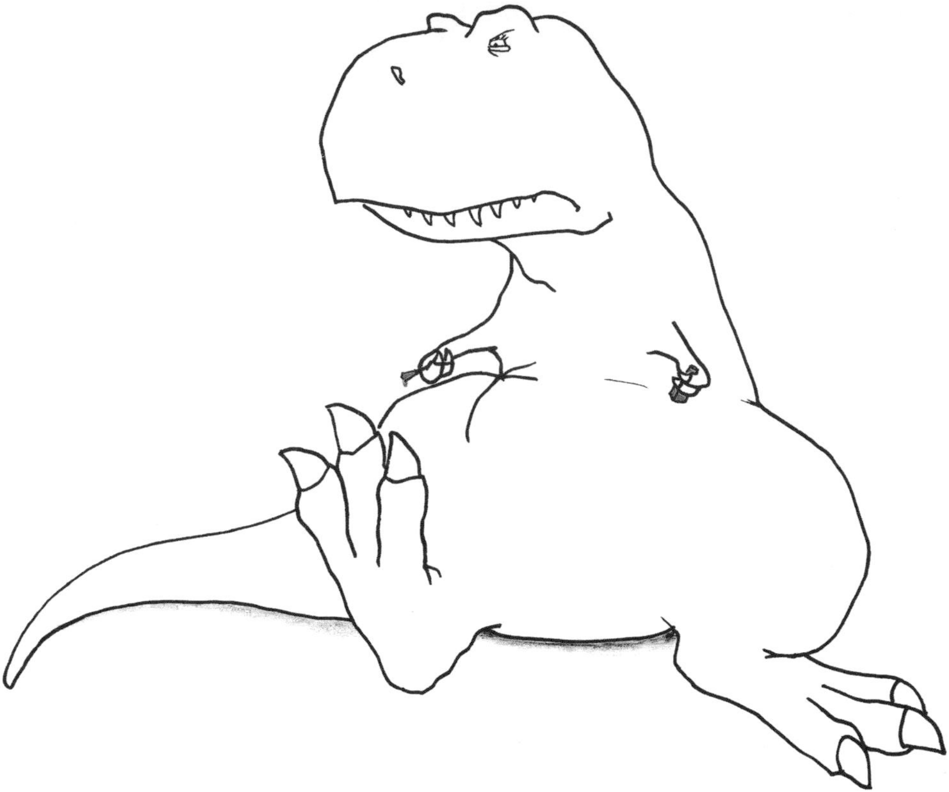

She-Rex trying to paint her toenails . . .

She-Rex trying to put on a bra . . .

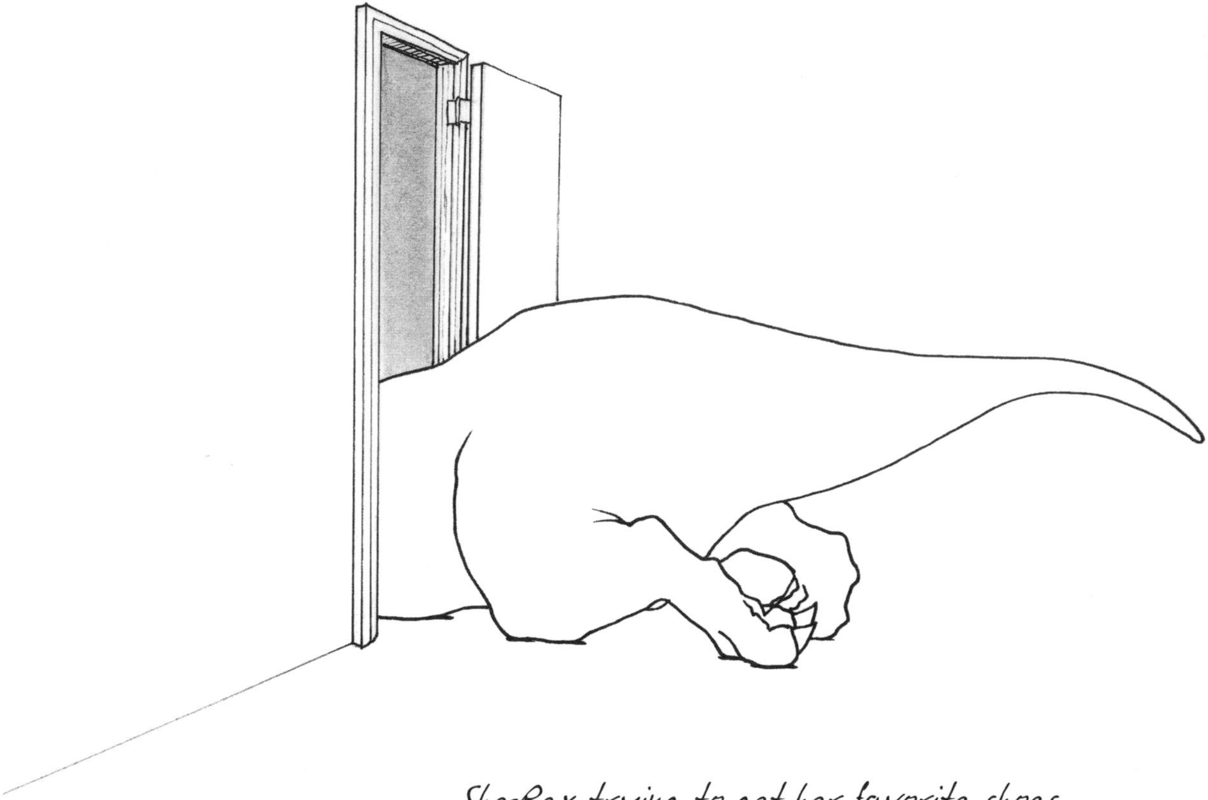

She-Rex trying to get her favorite shoes . . .

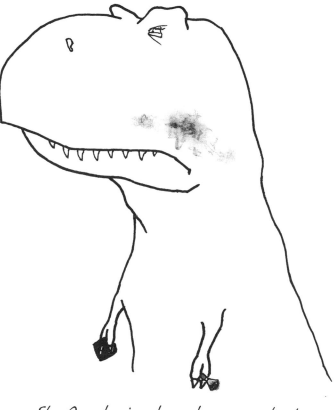

She-Rex trying to put on eye shadow . . .

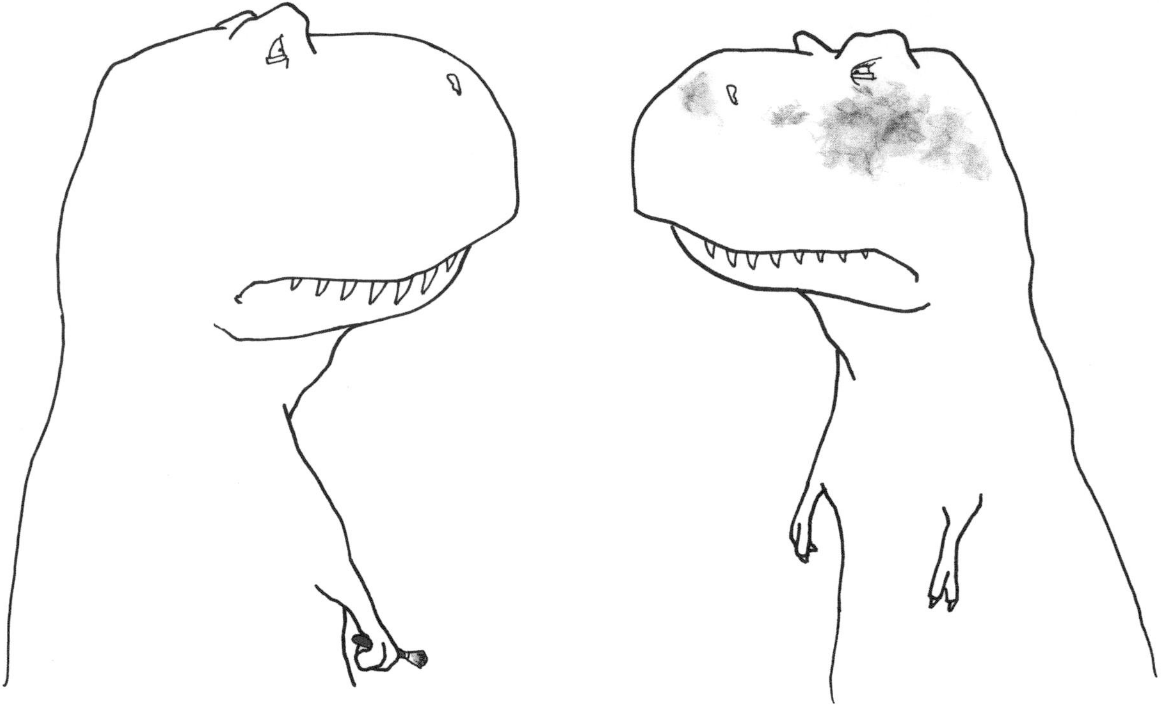

T-Rex trying to help She-Rex put on eye shadow . . .

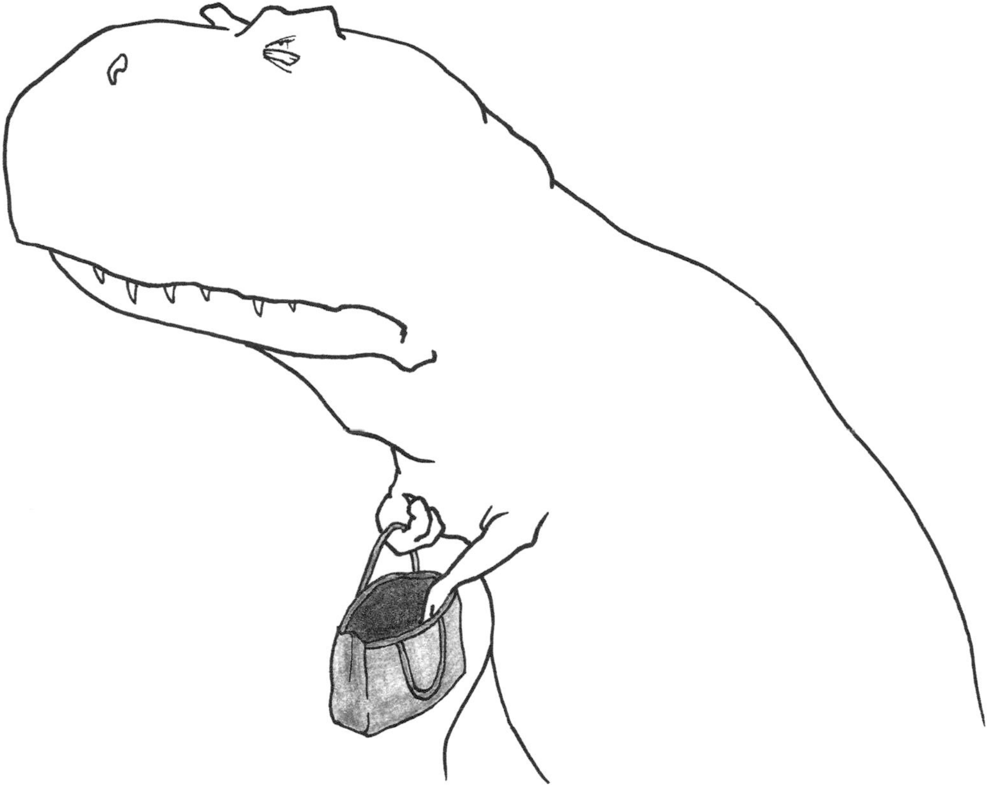

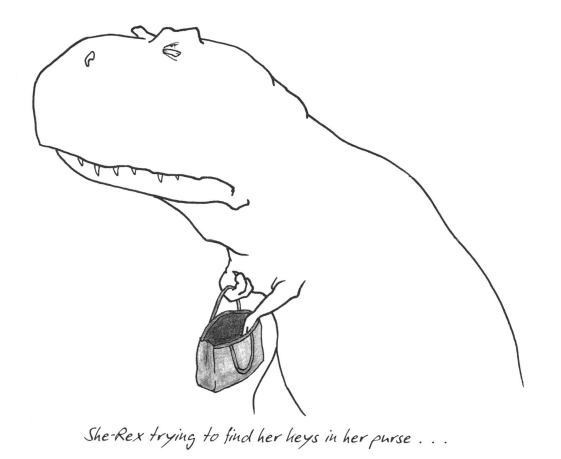

She-Rex trying to find her keys in her purse . . .

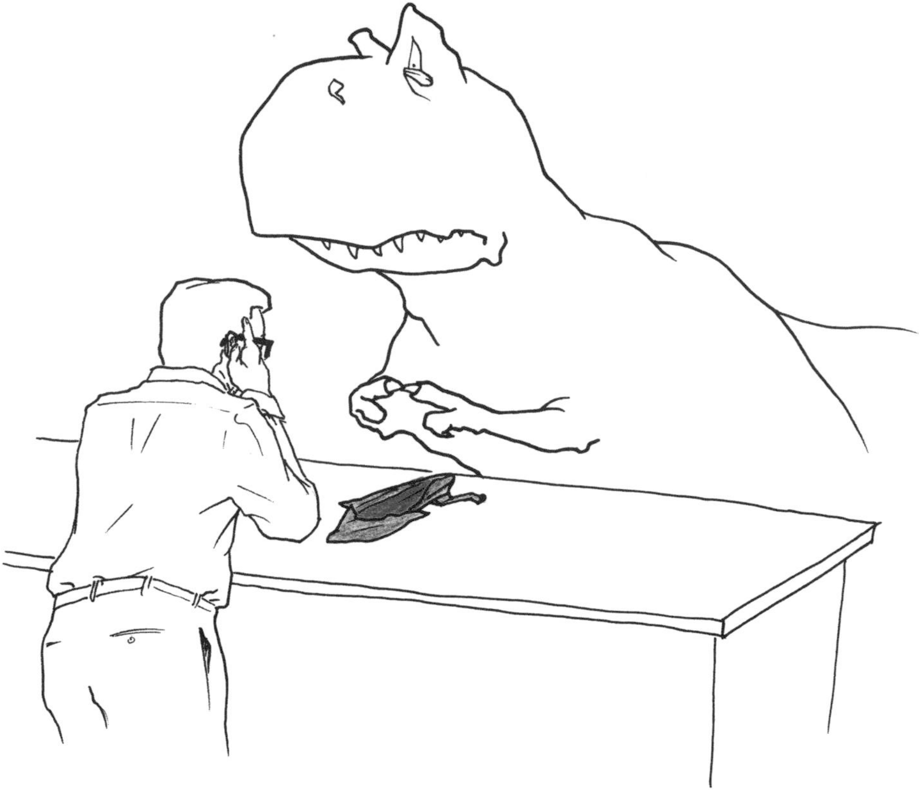

She-Rex trying to get her stiletto repaired . . .

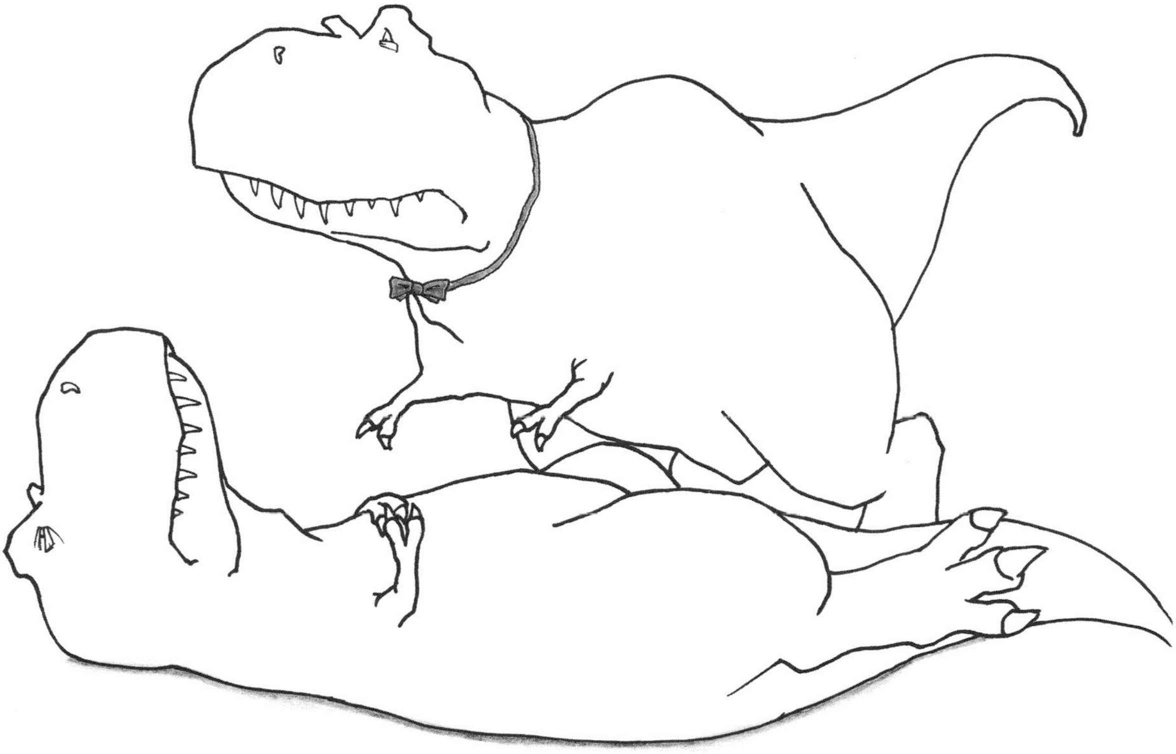

T-Rex trying to dip his dance partner . . .

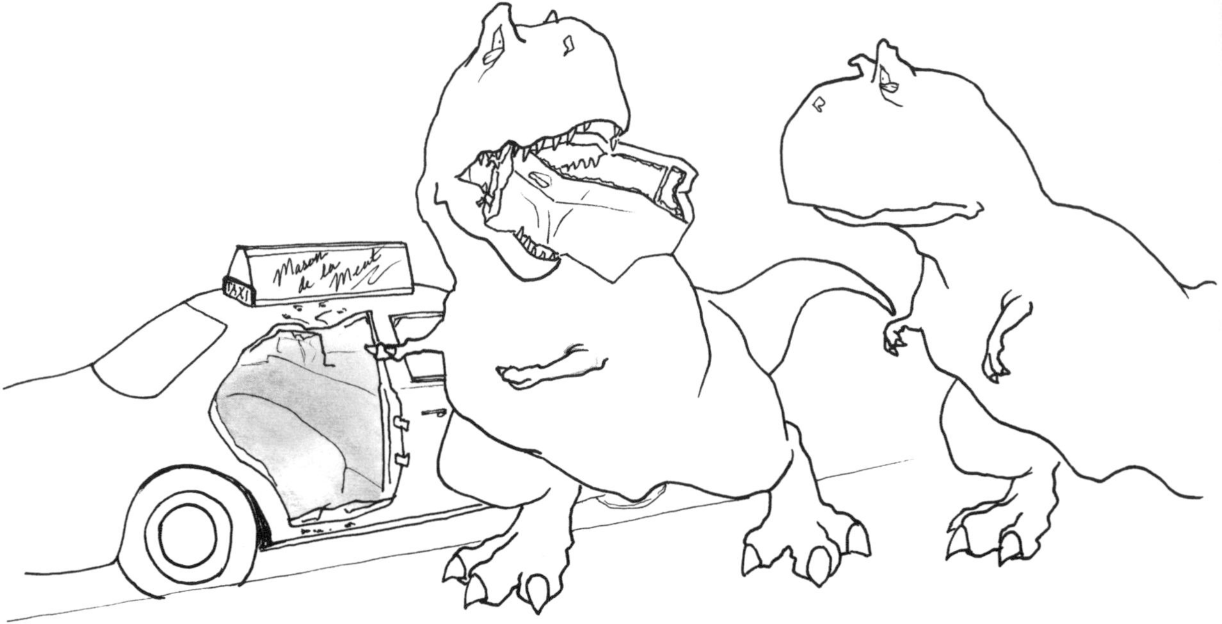
Mason de la Meat
TAXI

T-Rex trying to grab a cab for She-Rex . . .

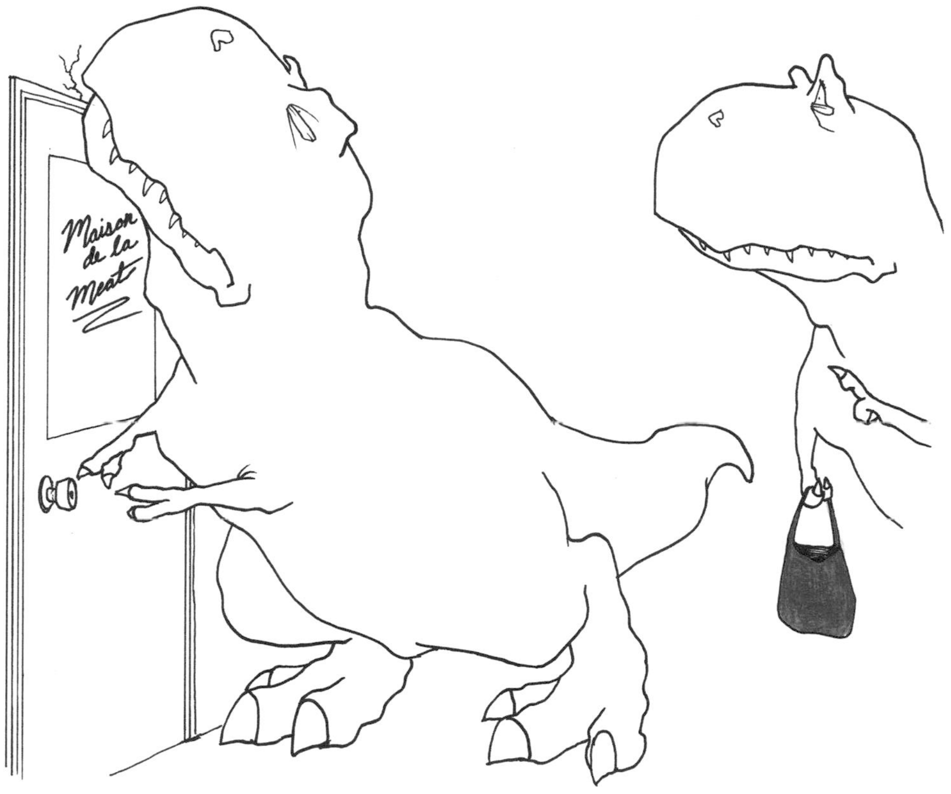
Maison de la Meat

T-Rex trying to open the door for She-Rex . . .

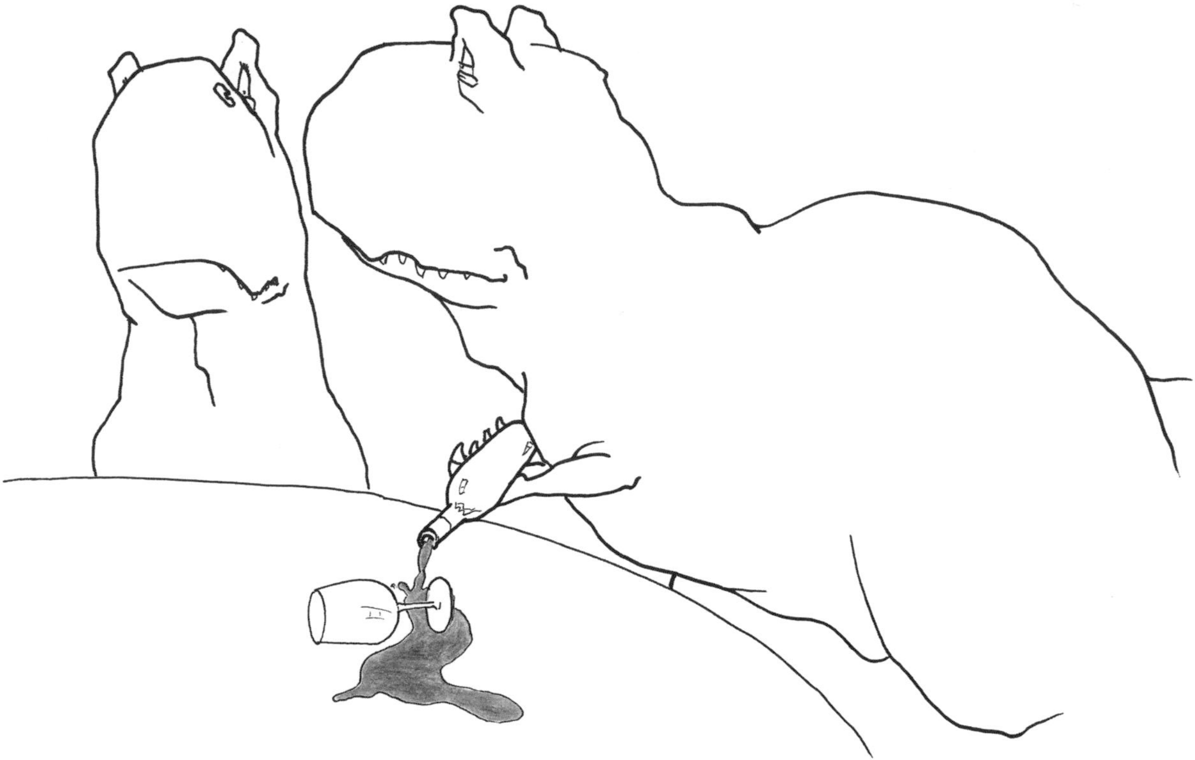

T-Rex trying to pour She-Rex a glass of wine . . .

She-Rex trying to catch the bouquet at a wedding . . .

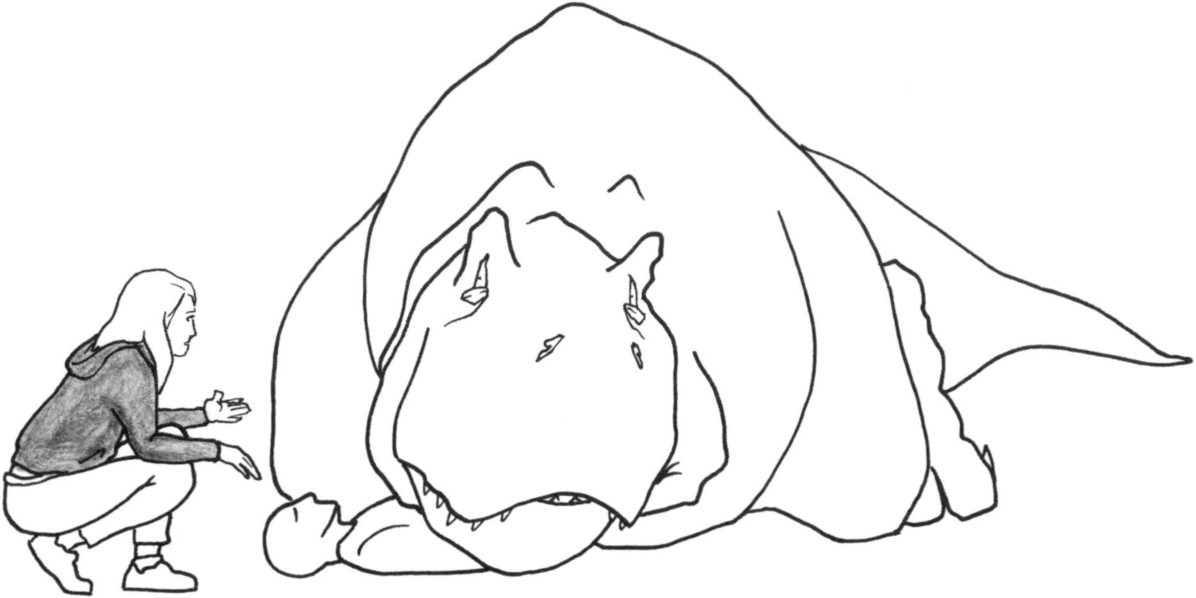

T-Rex trying to learn CPR . . .

T-Rex trying to tell everyone he's choking . . .

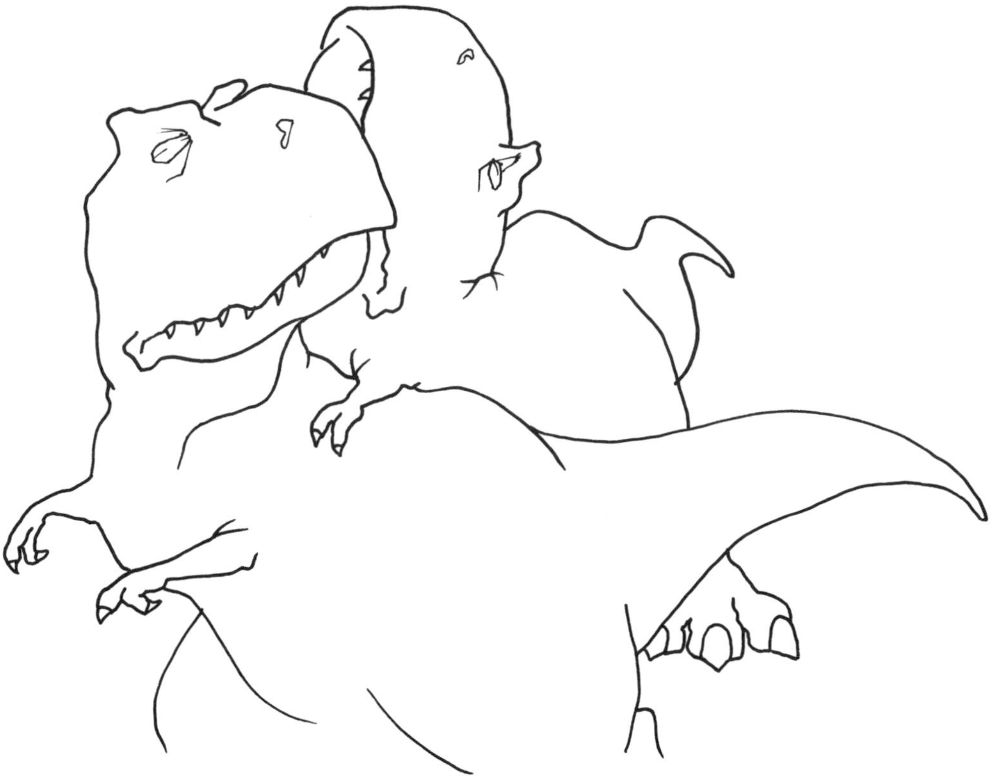

She-Rex trying to perform the Heimlich on T-Rex . . .

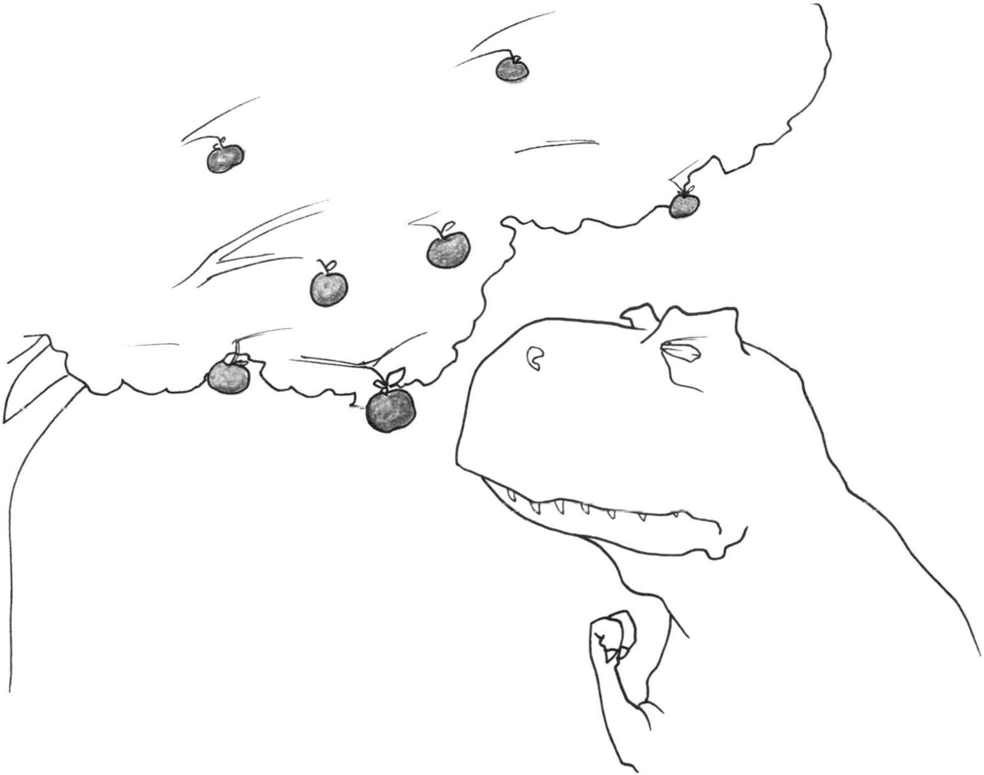

T-Rex trying to grab the low-hanging fruit . . .

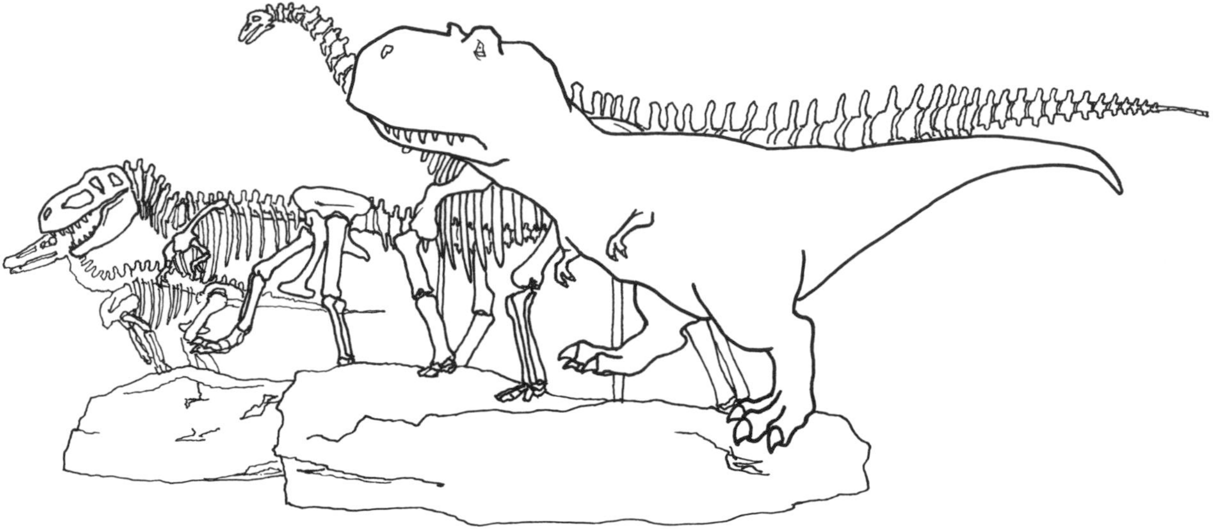

T-Rex trying to fit in . . .

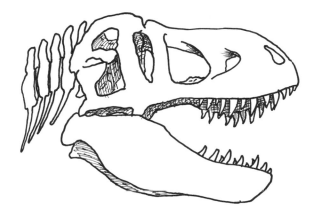

T-Rex trying to reconnect . . .

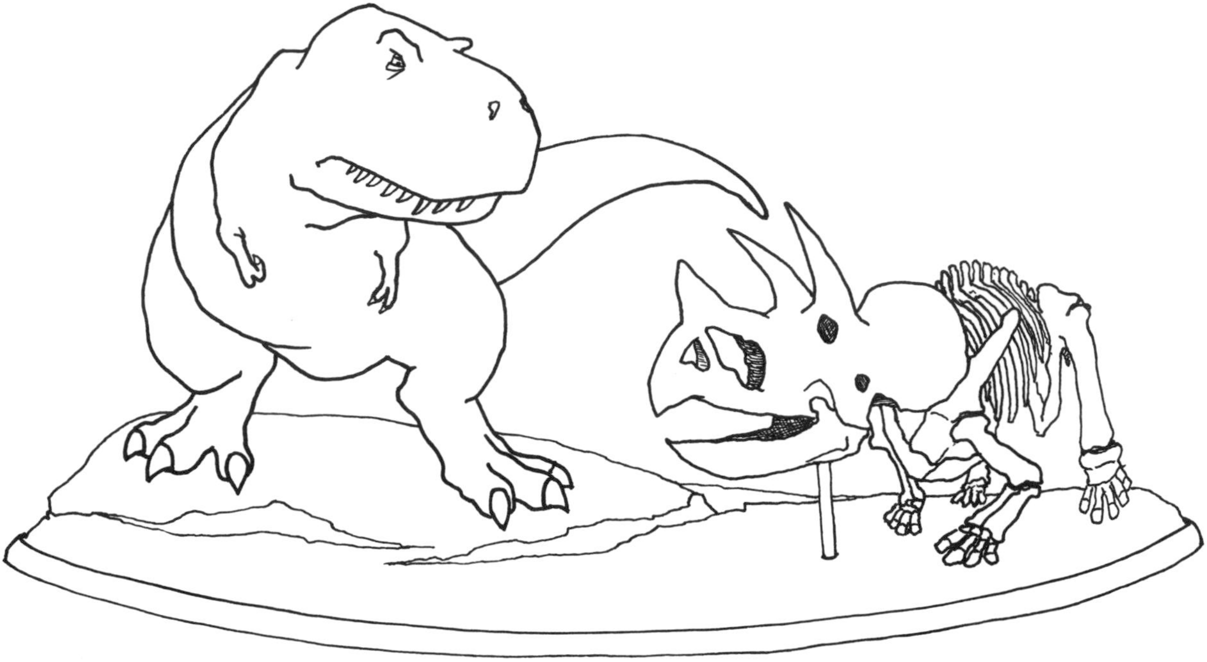

T-Rex trying to settle an old score . . .

T-Rex trying to raise awareness for prehistoric extinctions . . .

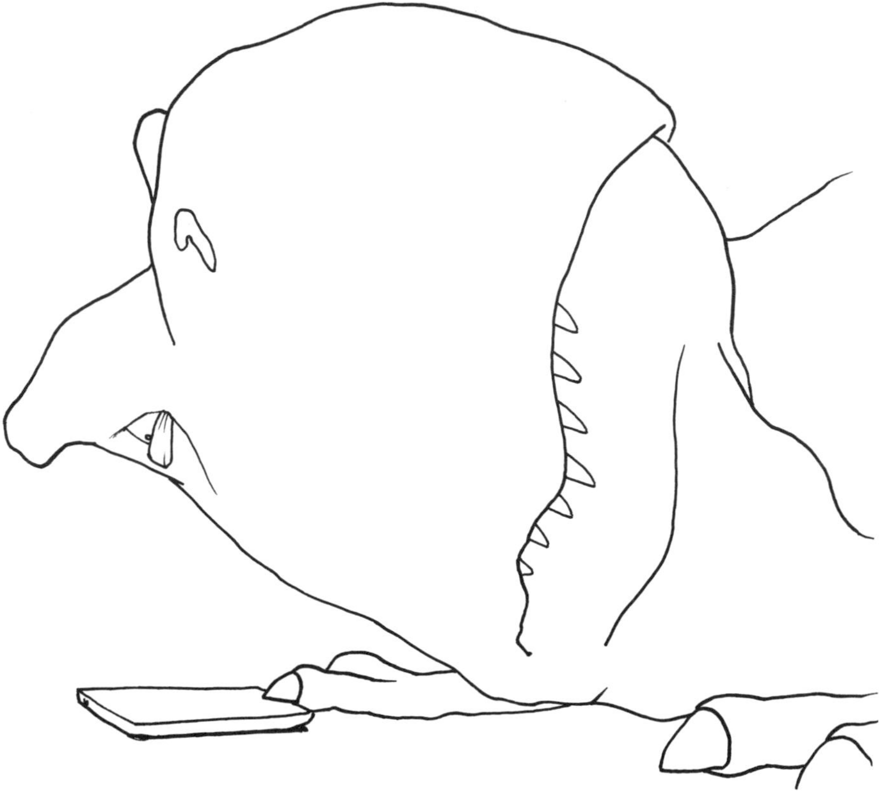

T-Rex trying to read his e-mail . . .

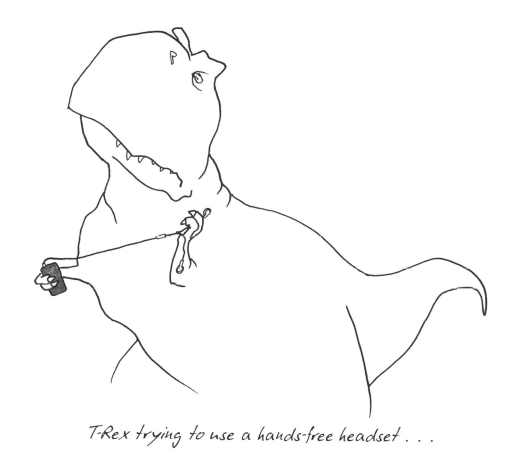

T-Rex trying to use a hands-free headset . . .

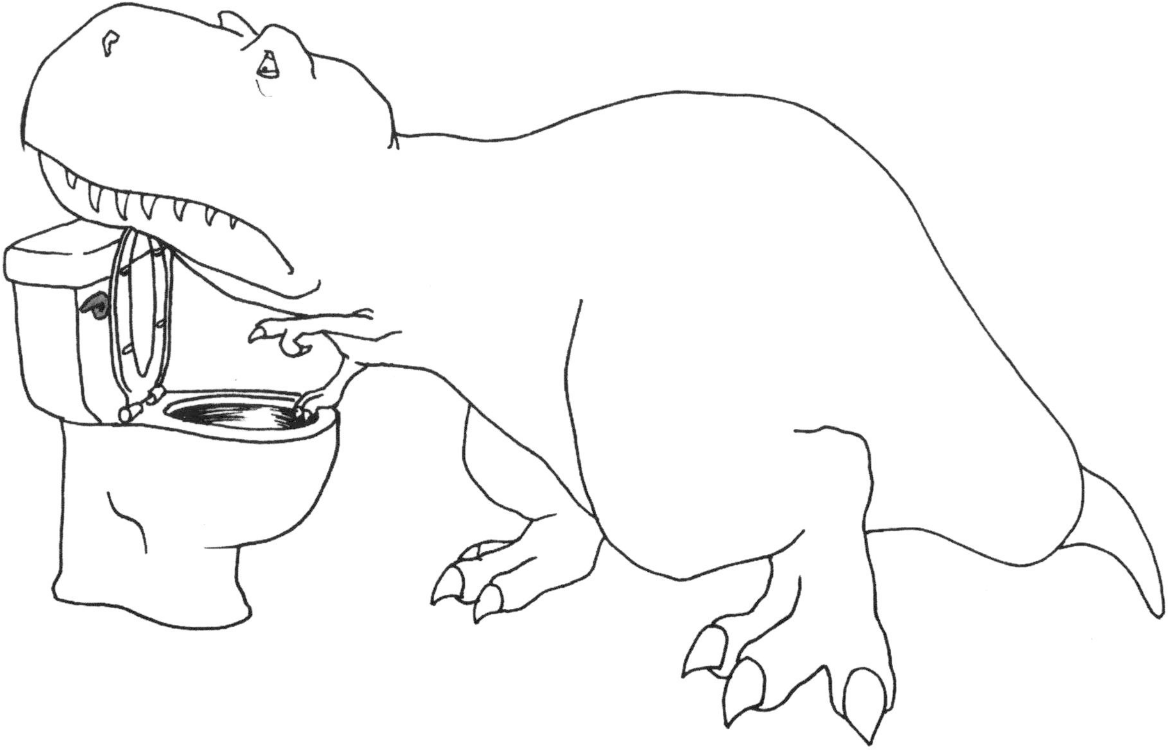

T-Rex trying to weather the stomach flu . . .

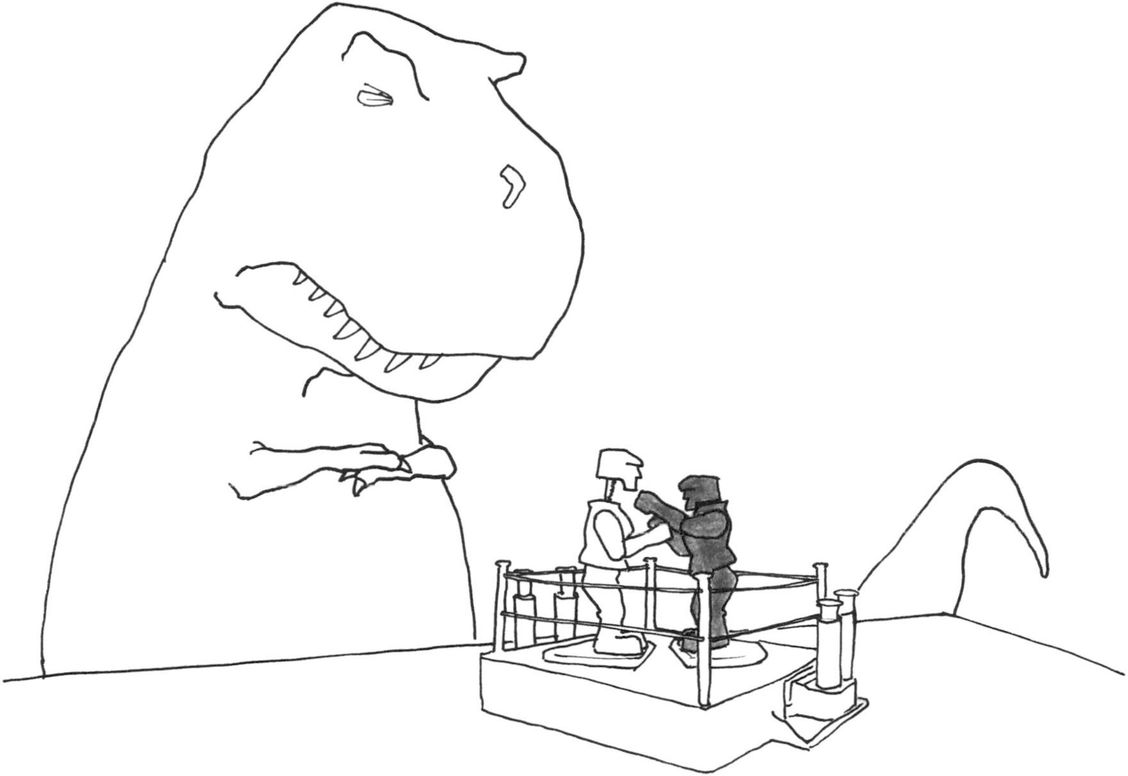

T-Rex trying to play Rock 'em Sock 'em Robots . . .

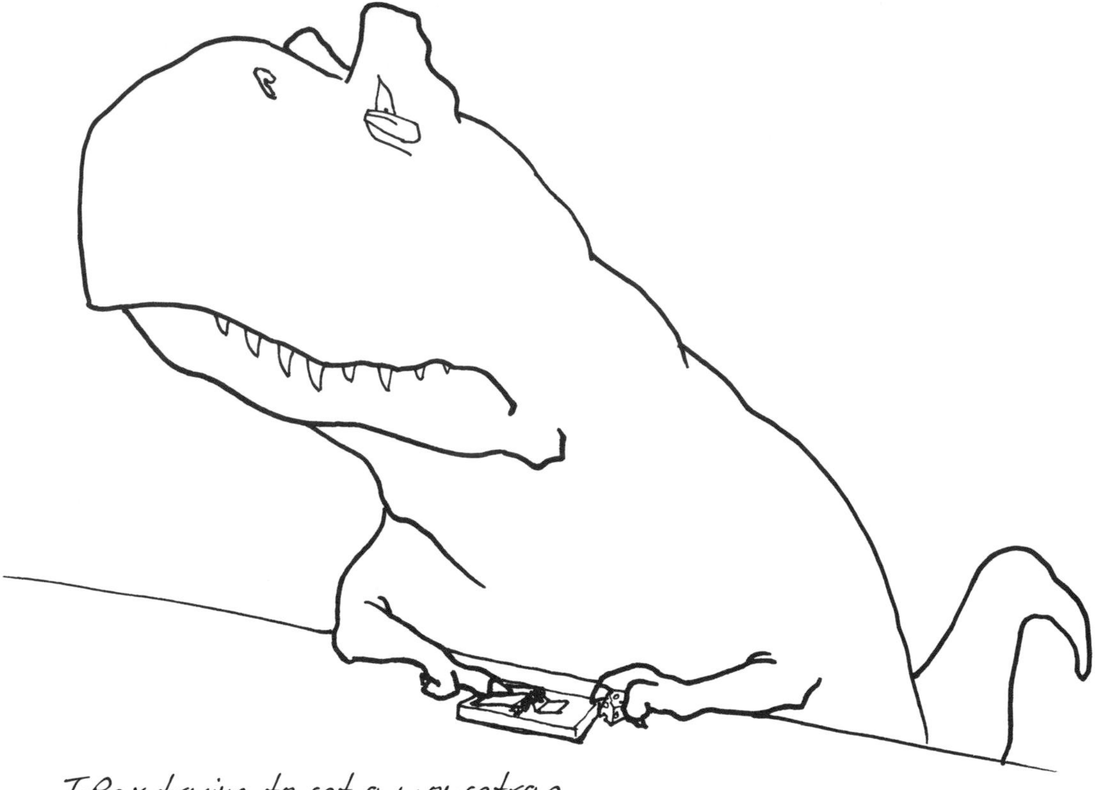

T-Rex trying to set a mousetrap . . .

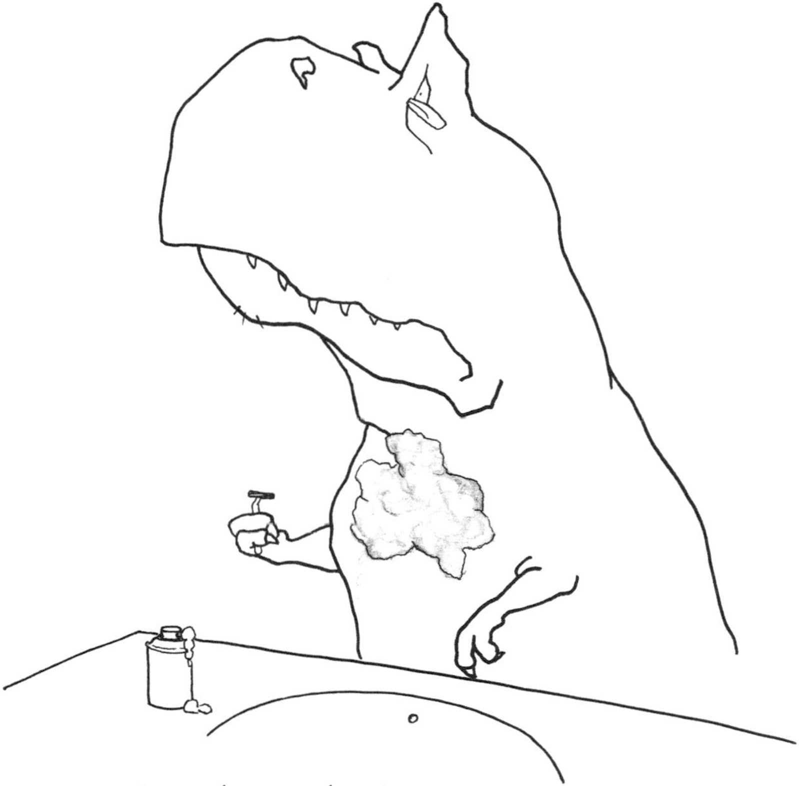

T-Rex trying to shave . . .

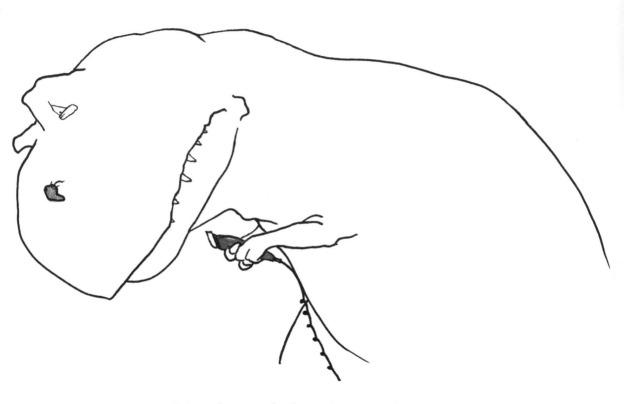

T-Rex trying to trim his nose hairs . . .

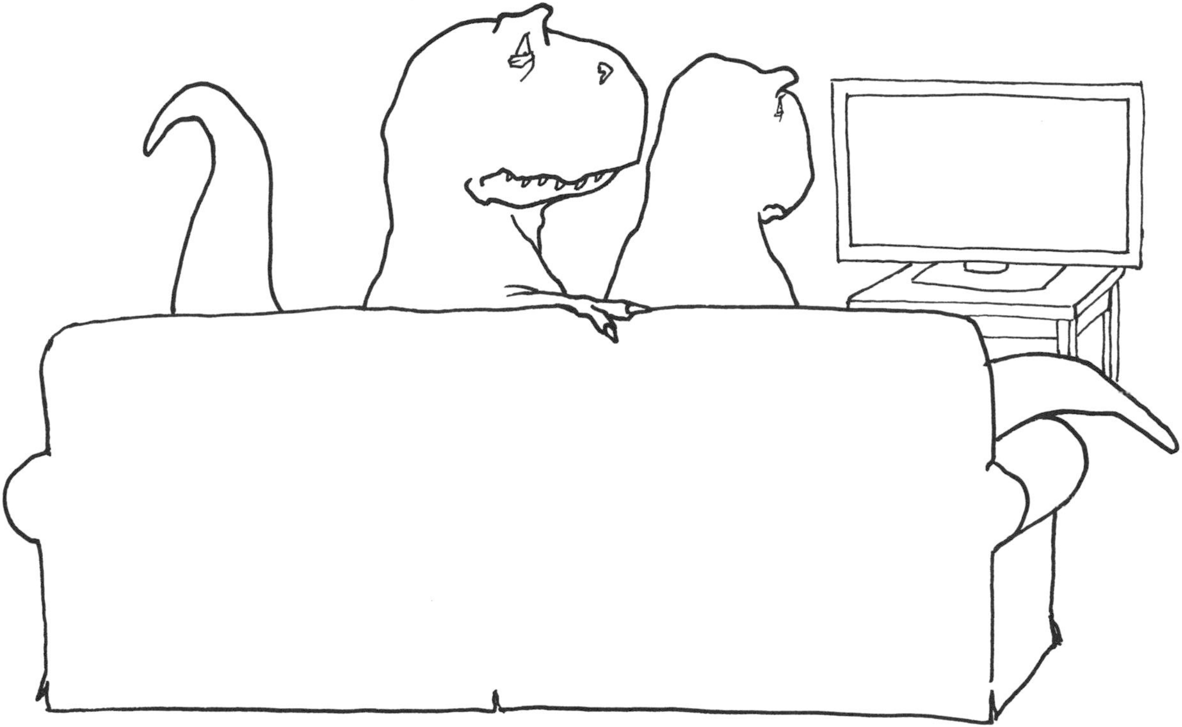

T-Rex trying to make a move while watching a movie . . .

T-Rex trying to spoon She-Rex . . .

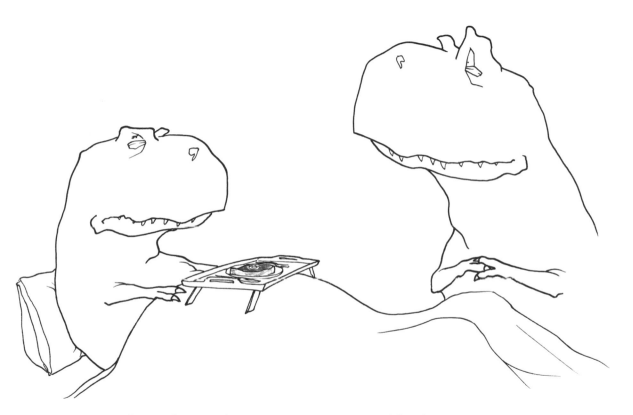

T-Rex trying to serve She-Rex breakfast in bed . . .

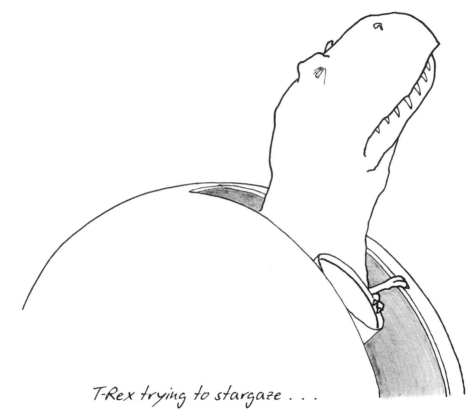

T-Rex trying to stargaze . . .

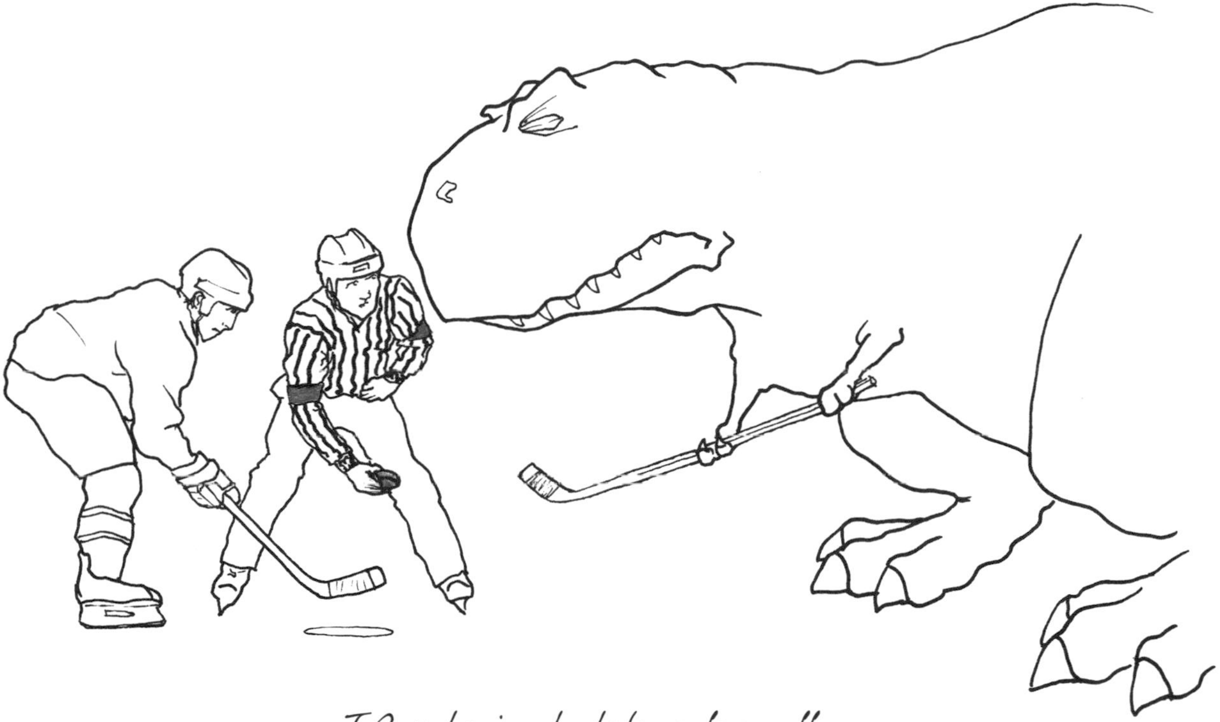

T-Rex trying to take a face-off . . .

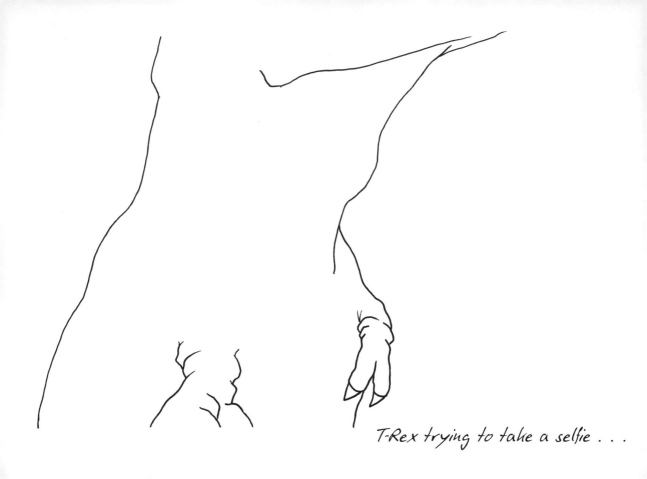

T-Rex trying to take a selfie . . .

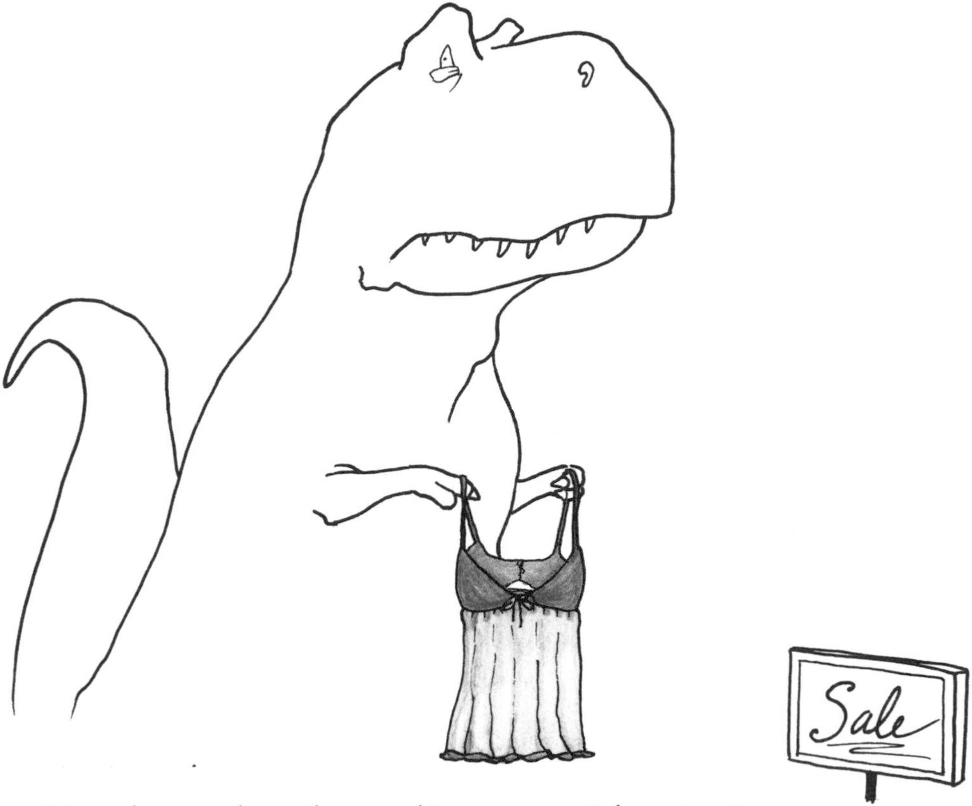
Sale

T-Rex trying to get something special for She-Rex . . .

T-Rex trying to teach She-Rex how to make pottery . . .

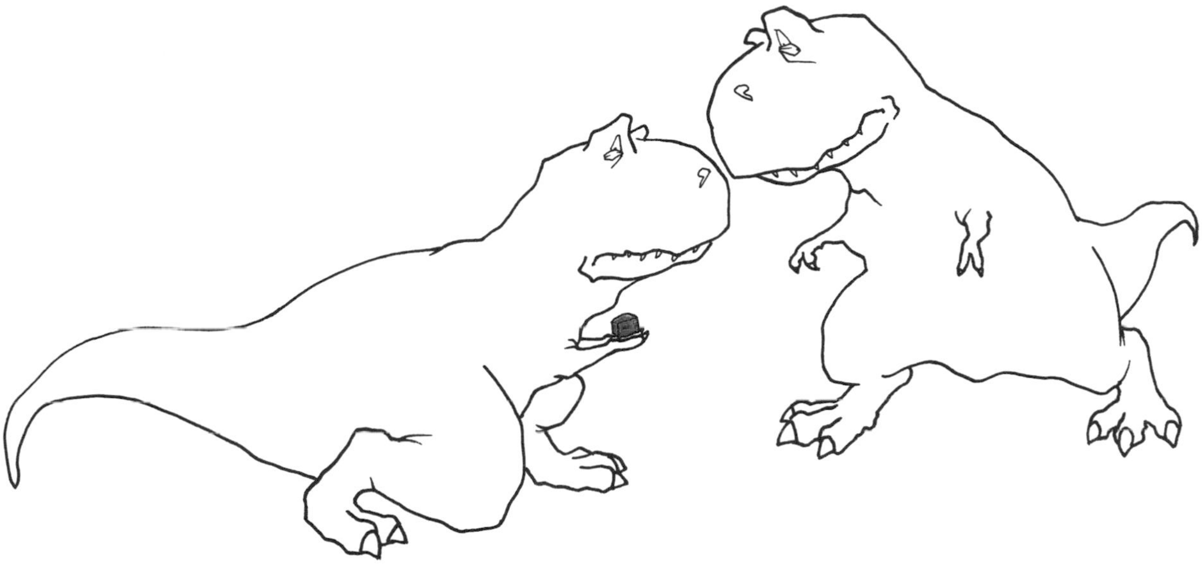

T-Rex trying to propose to She-Rex . . .

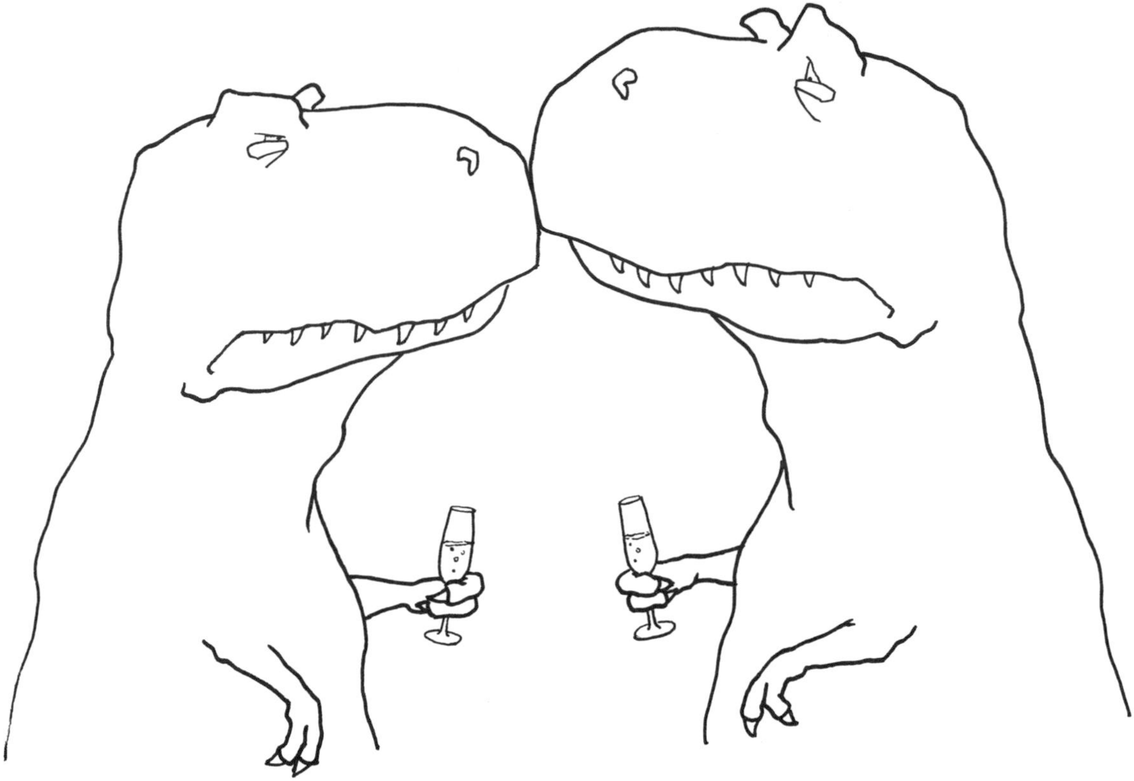

T-Rex trying to toast with She-Rex . . .

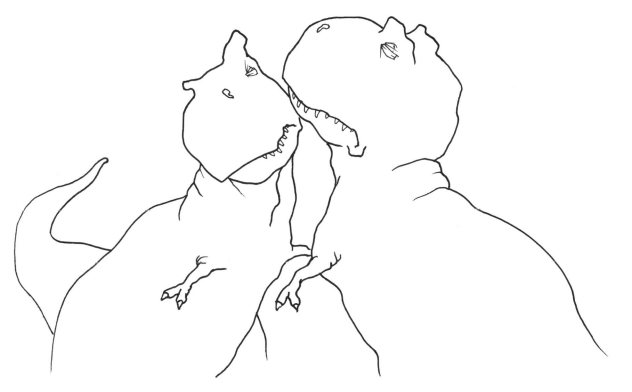

T-Rexes trying to chest bump . . .

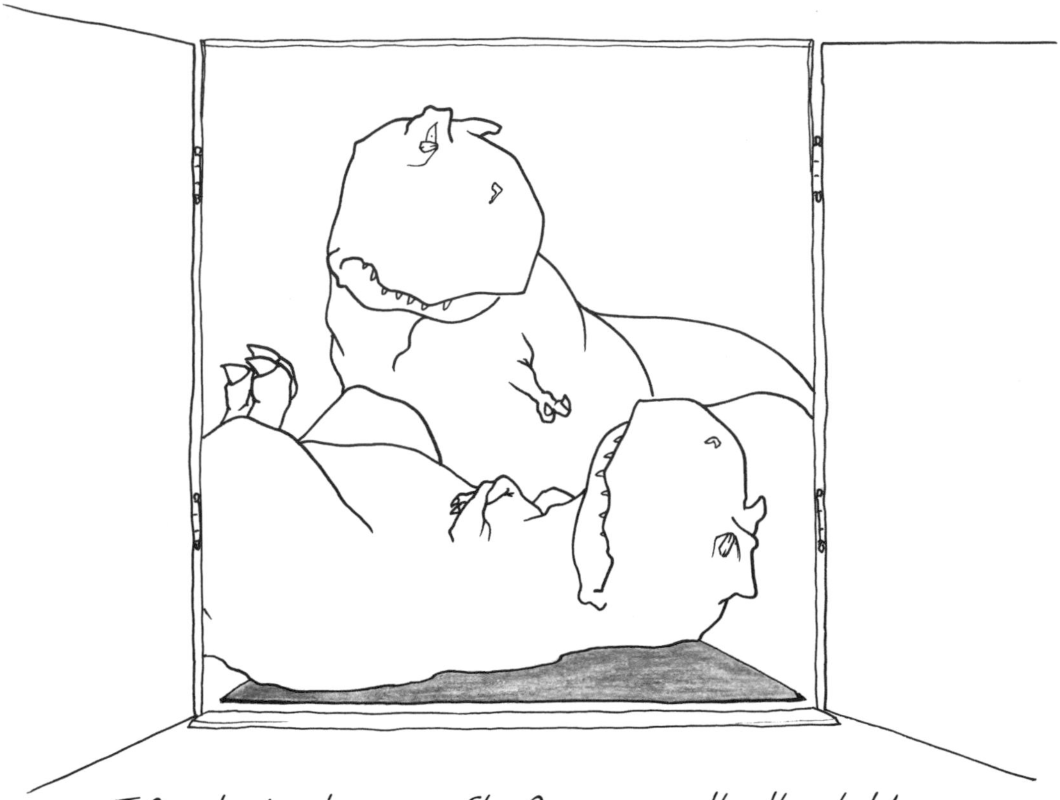

T-Rex trying to carry She-Rex across the threshold . . .

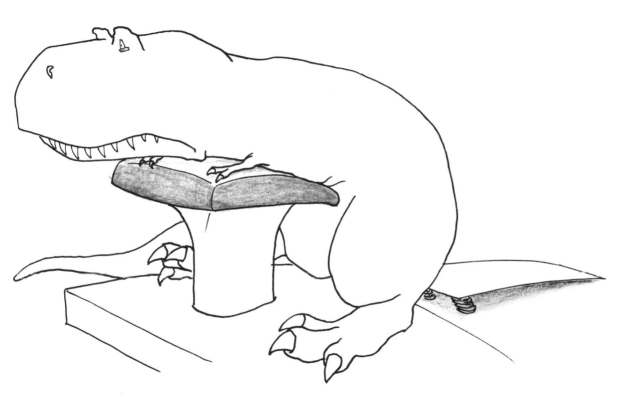

T-Rex trying to vault . . .

T-Rex trying to win a sack race . . .

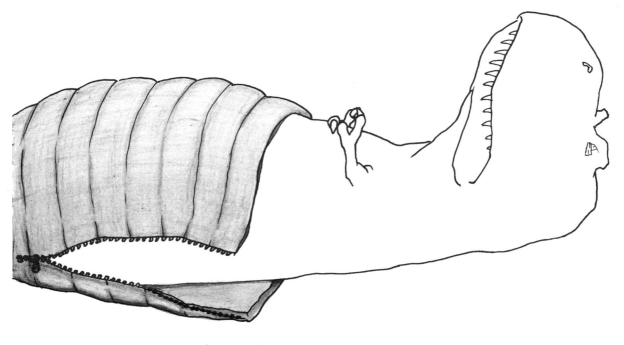

T-Rex trying to zip up his sleeping bag . . .

T-Rex trying to shovel his driveway . . .

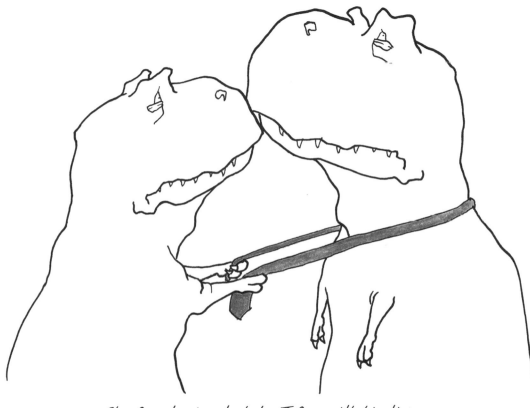

She-Rex trying to help T-Rex with his tie . . .

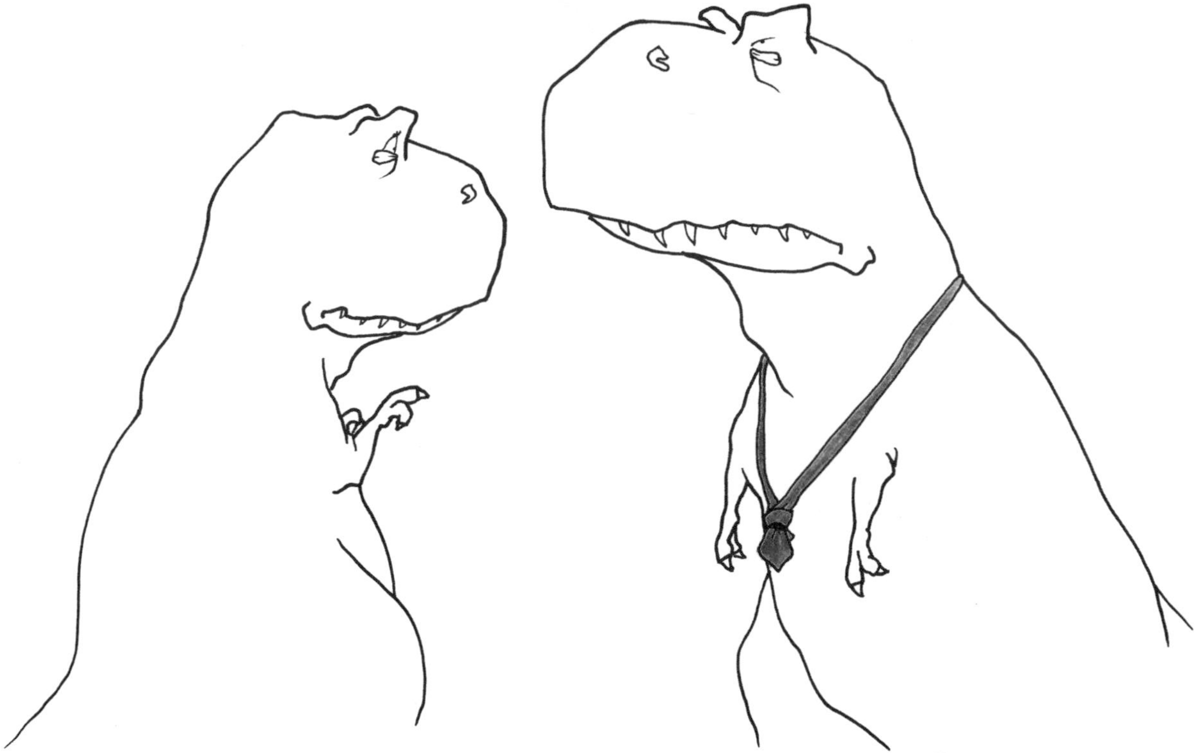

She-Rex trying to help T-Rex with his tie . . .

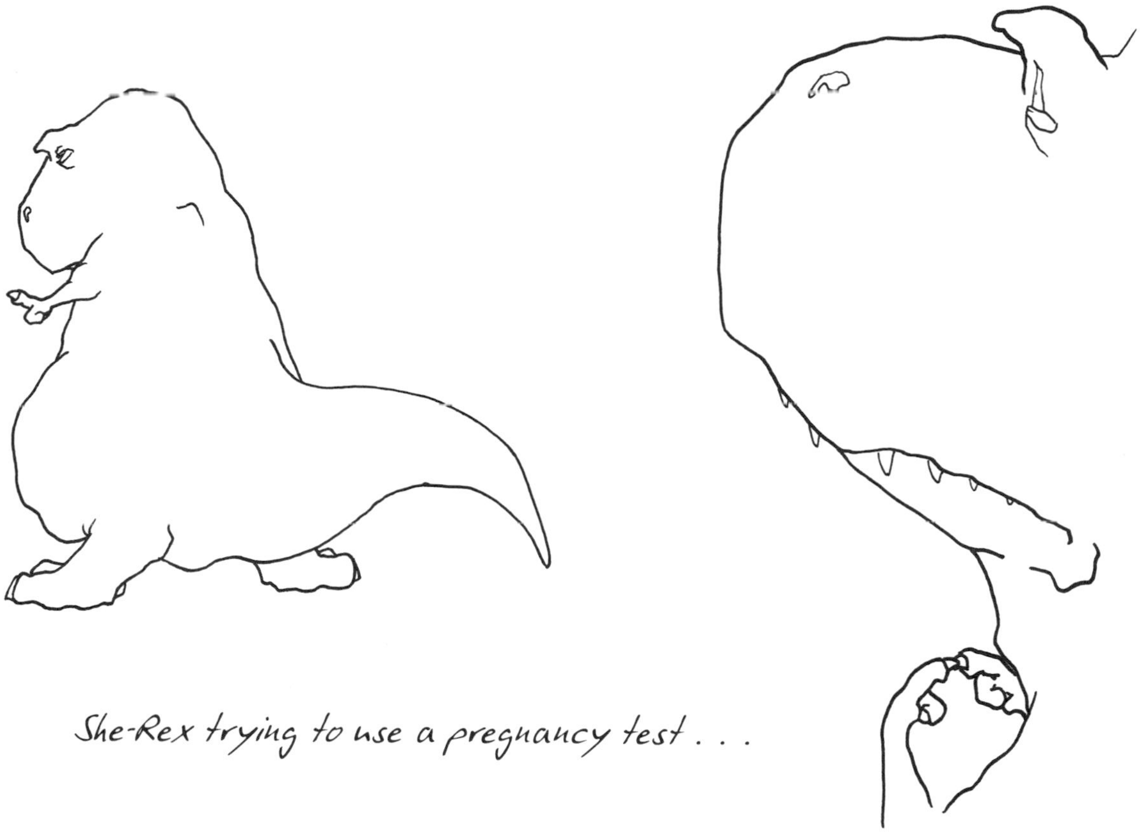

She-Rex trying to use a pregnancy test . . .

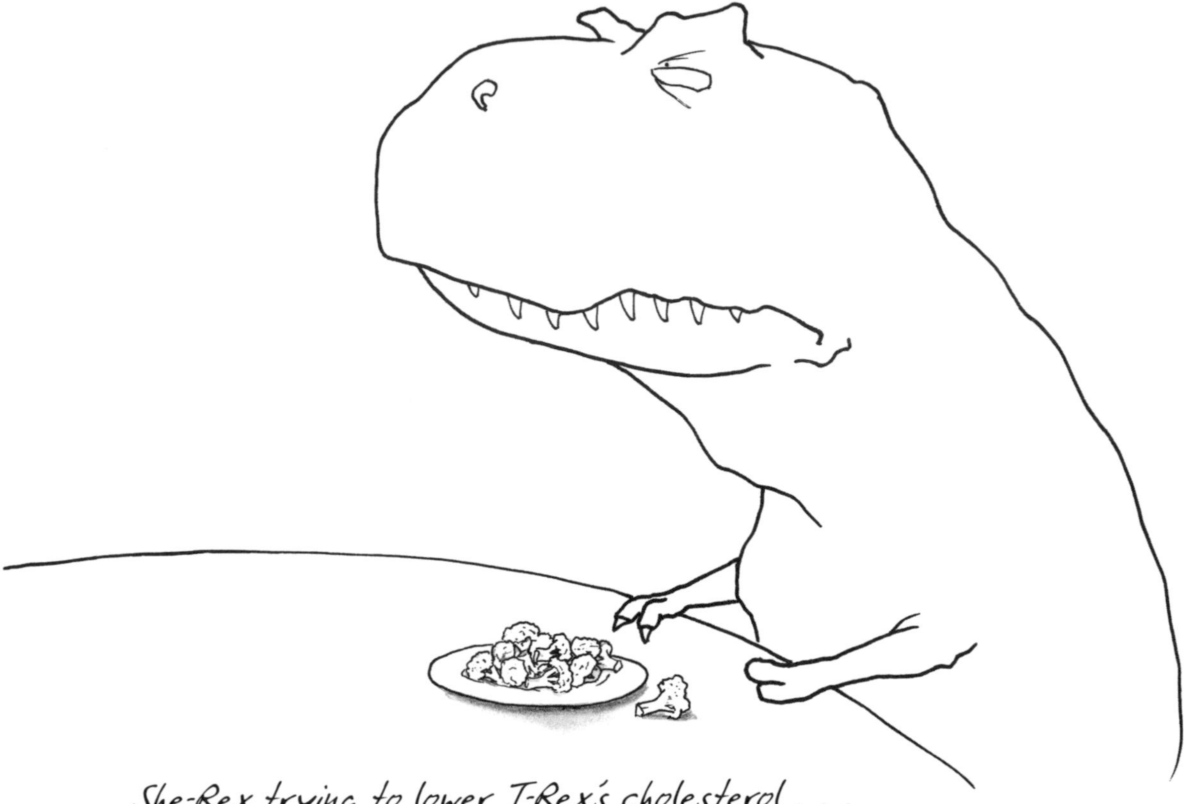

She-Rex trying to lower T-Rex's cholesterol . . .

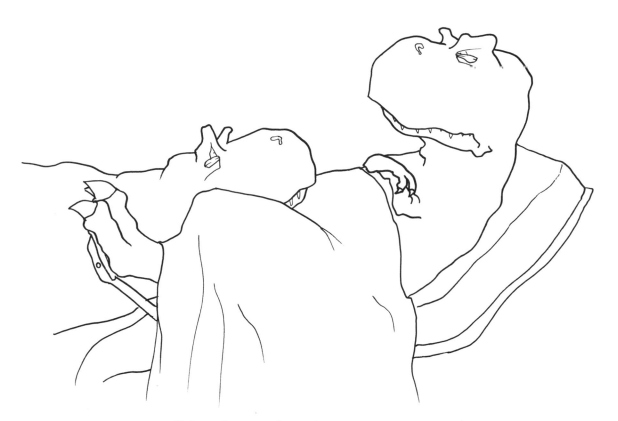

T-Rex trying to deliver Wee-Rex . . .

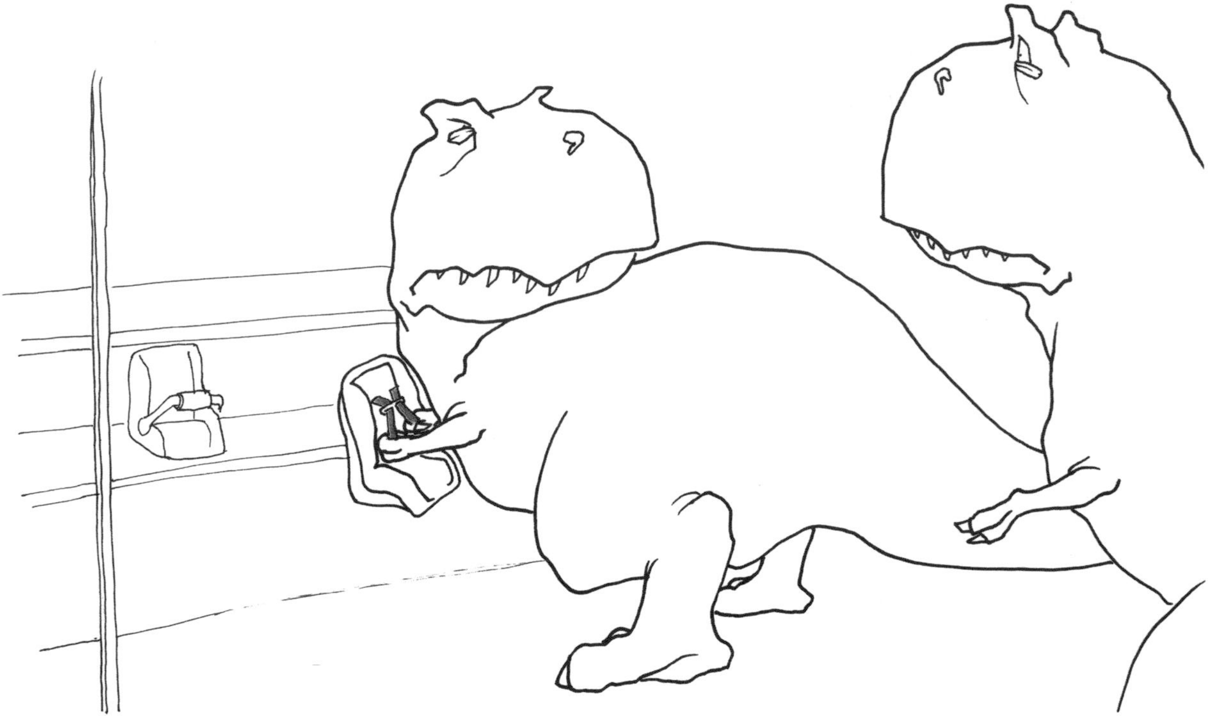

T-Rex and She-Rex trying to shop for car seats . . .

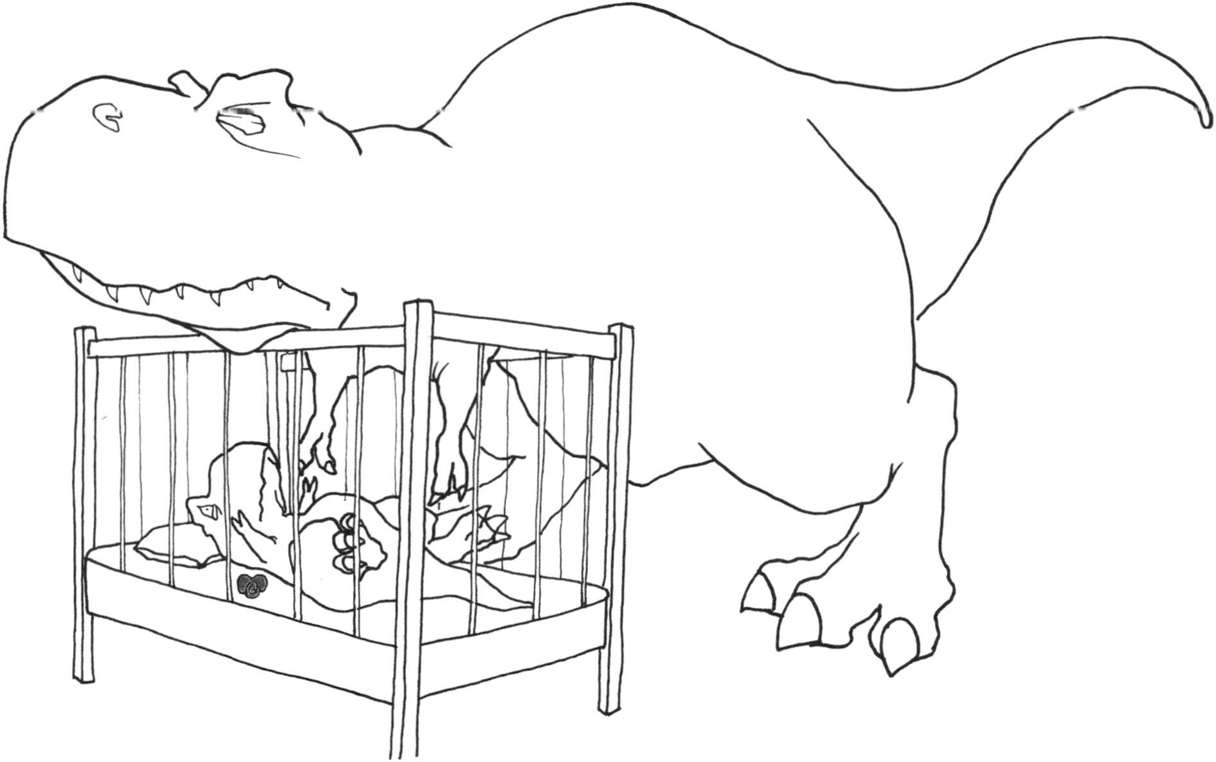

T-Rex trying to get Wee-Rex out of his crib . . .

T-Rex trying to change Wee-Rex's diaper . . .

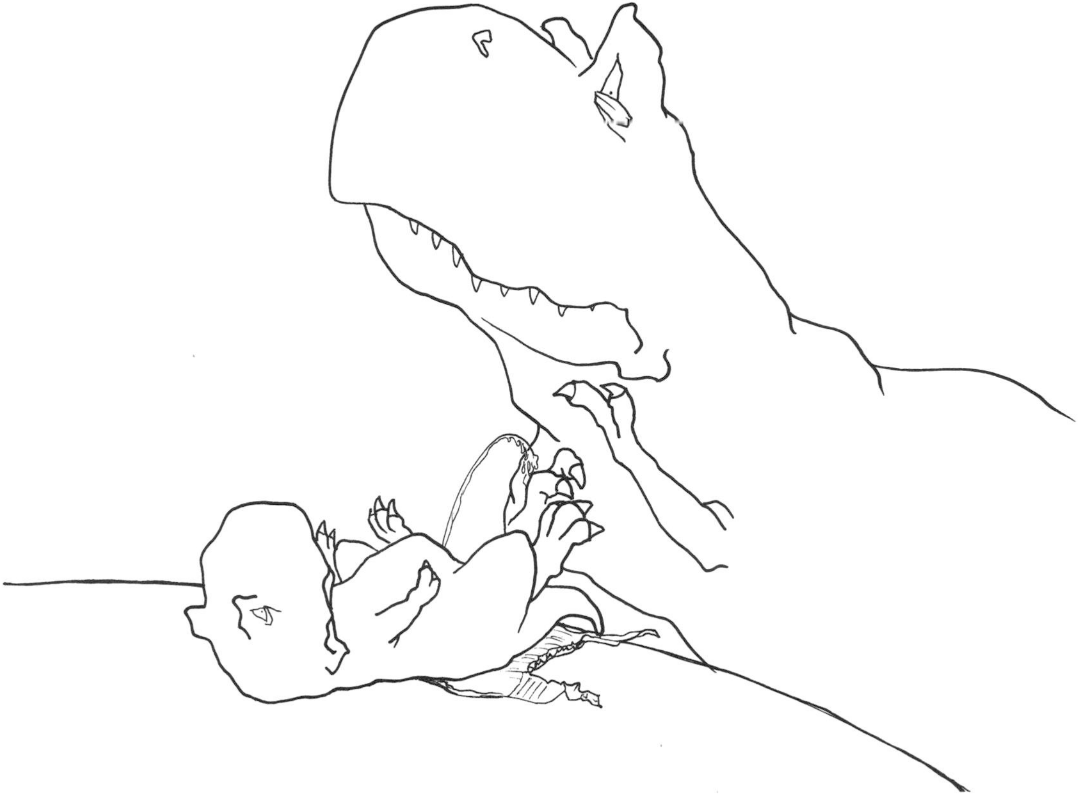

T-Rex trying to change Wee-Rex's diaper . . .

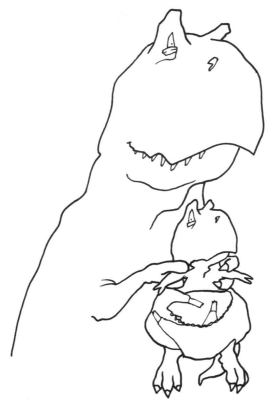

T-Rex trying to change Wee-Rex's diaper . . .

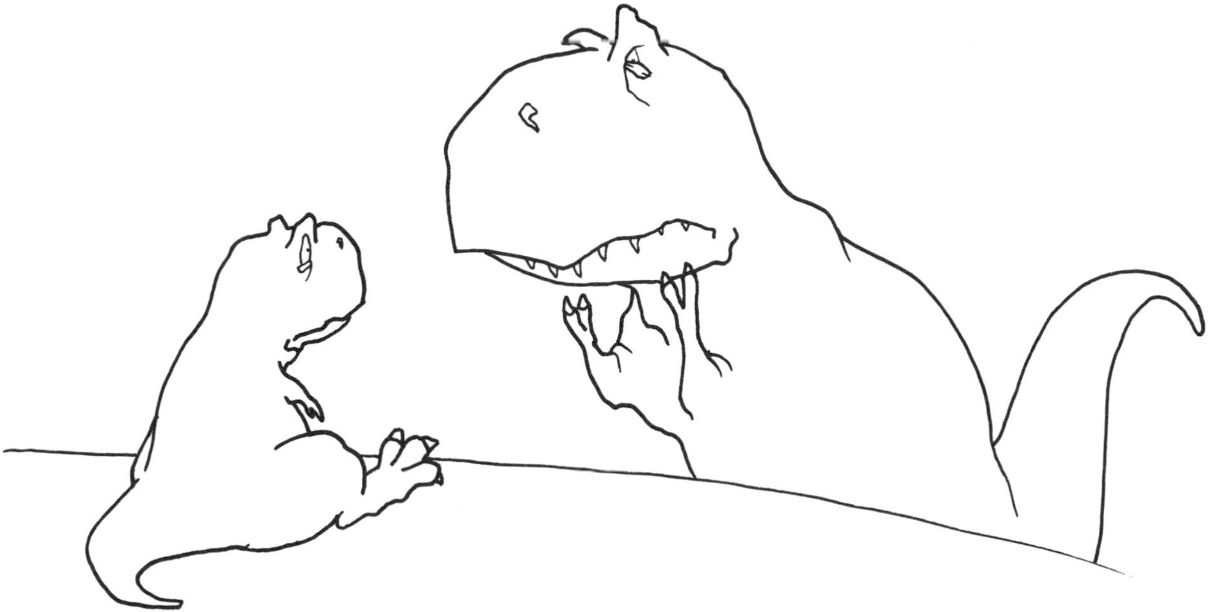

T-Rex trying to play peek-a-boo with Wee-Rex . . .

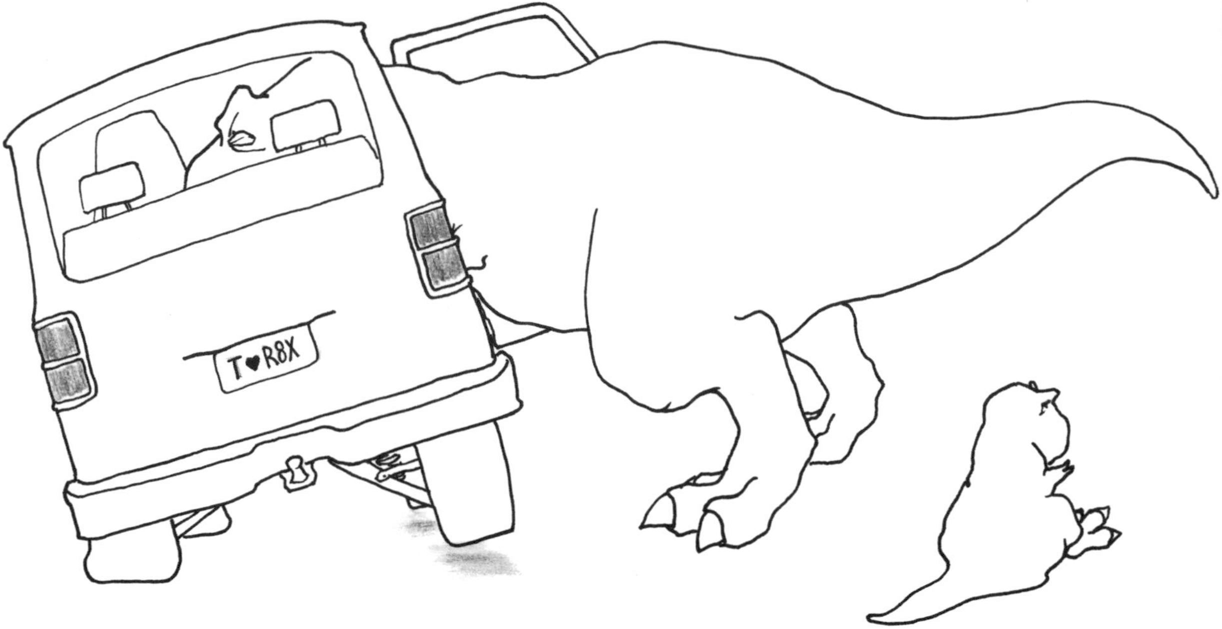
T♥R8X

T-Rex trying to install a car seat . . .

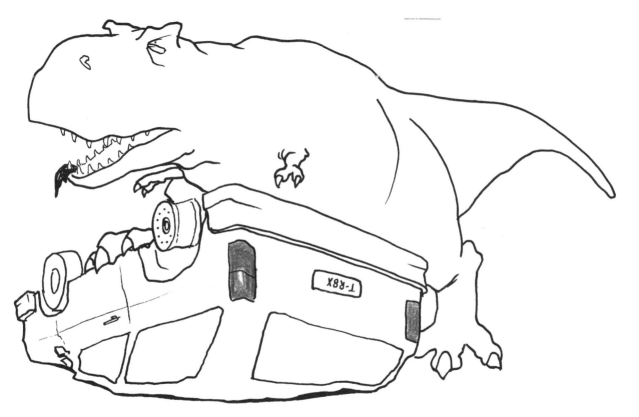

T-Rex trying to change a tire . . .

Wee-Rex trying to crawl . . .

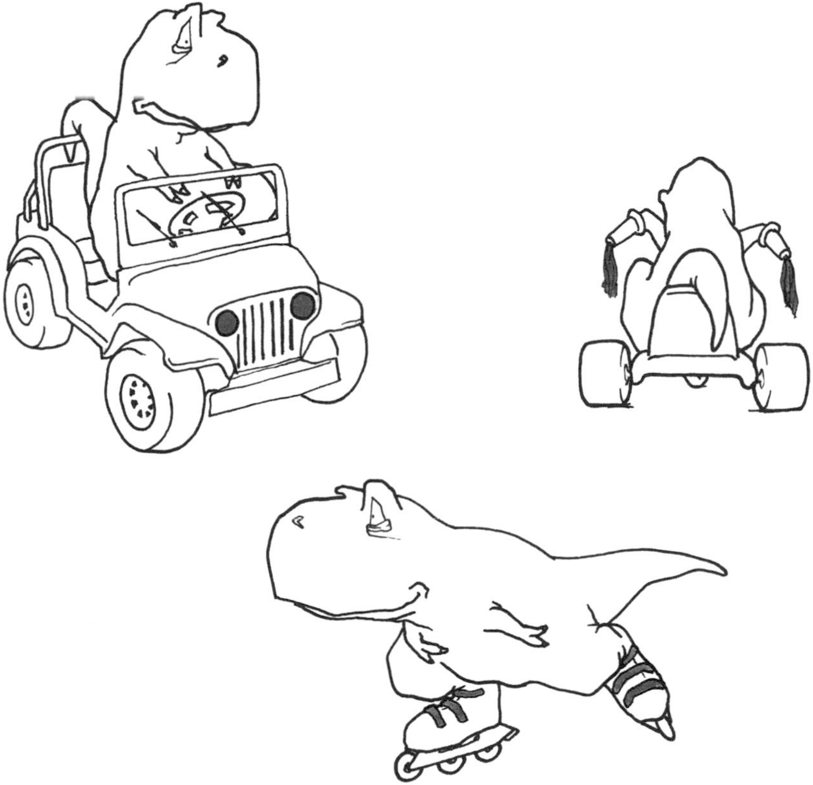

Wee-Rex trying to use his new power wheels . . . Big Wheel . . . ROLLERBLADES!!!

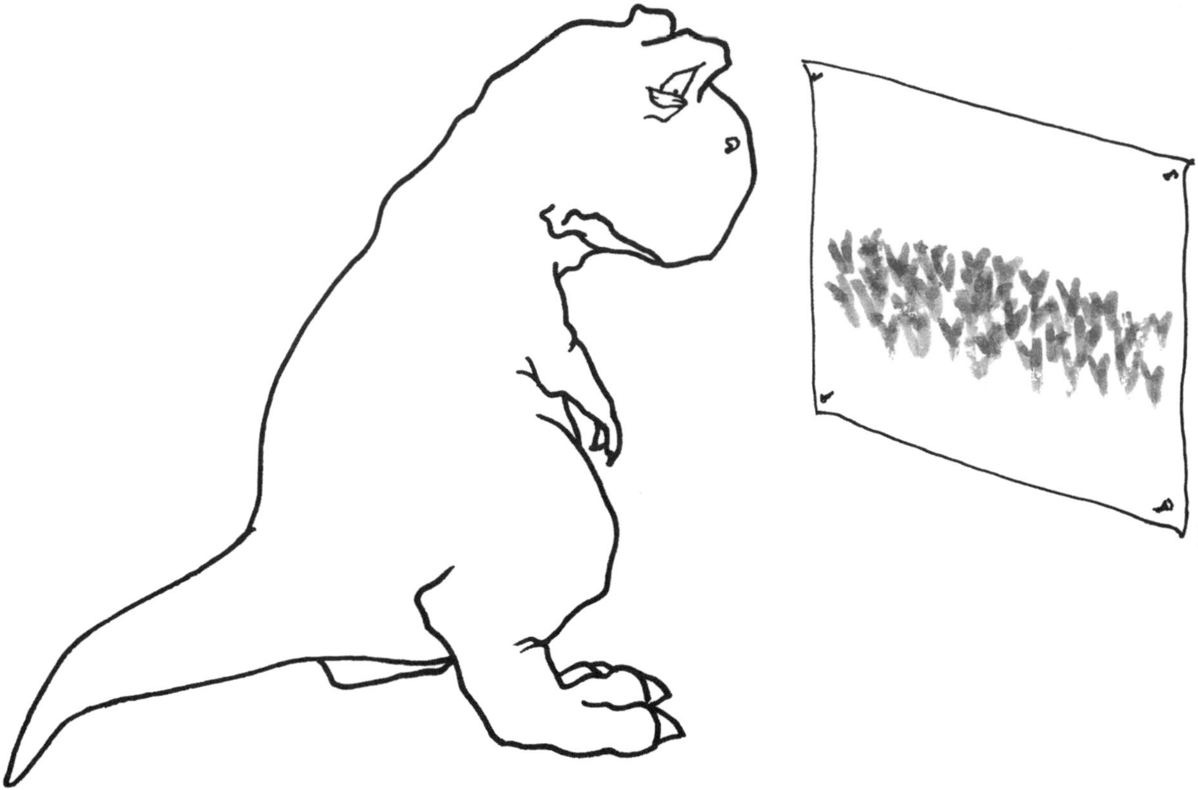

Wee-Rex trying to finger paint . . .

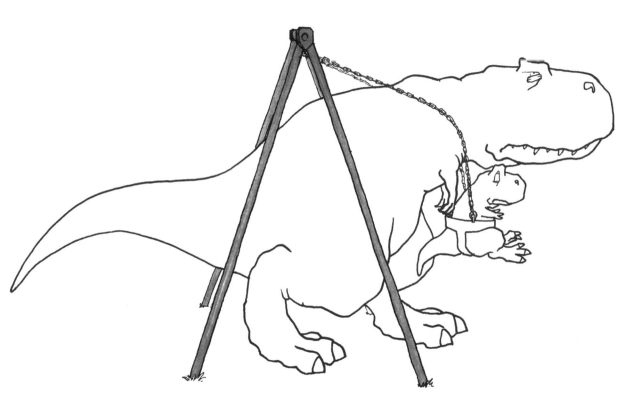

T-Rex trying to push Wee-Rex on a swing . . .

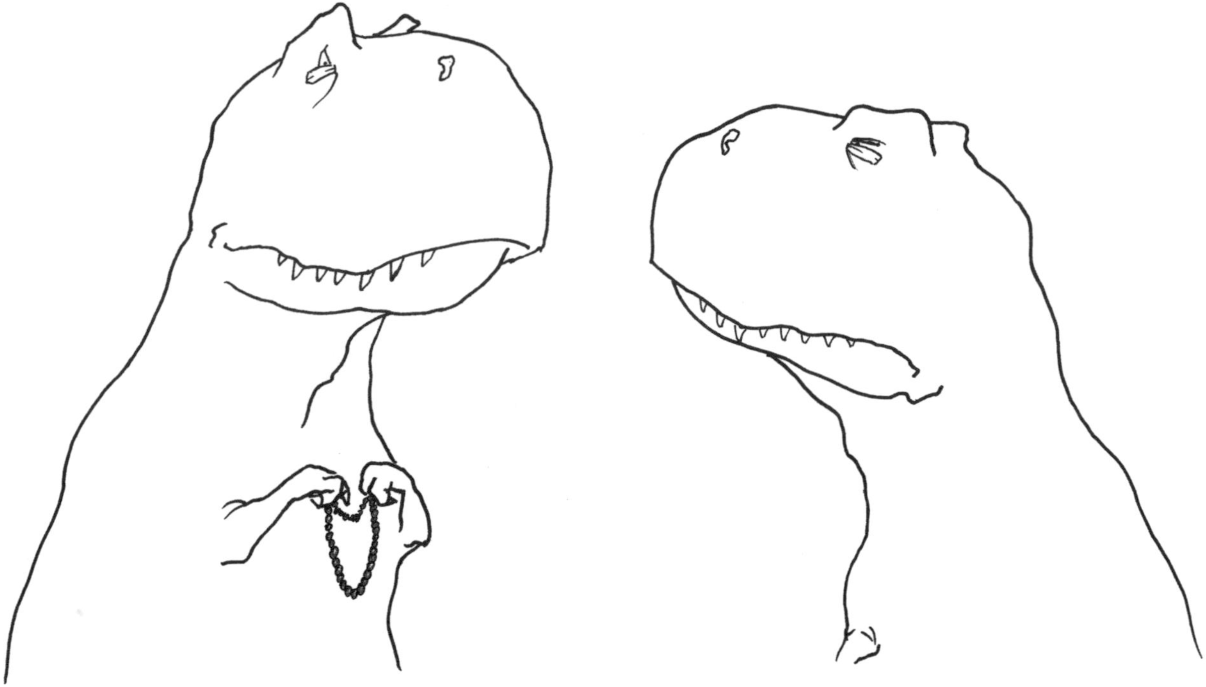

T-Rex trying to give She-Rex a gift . . .

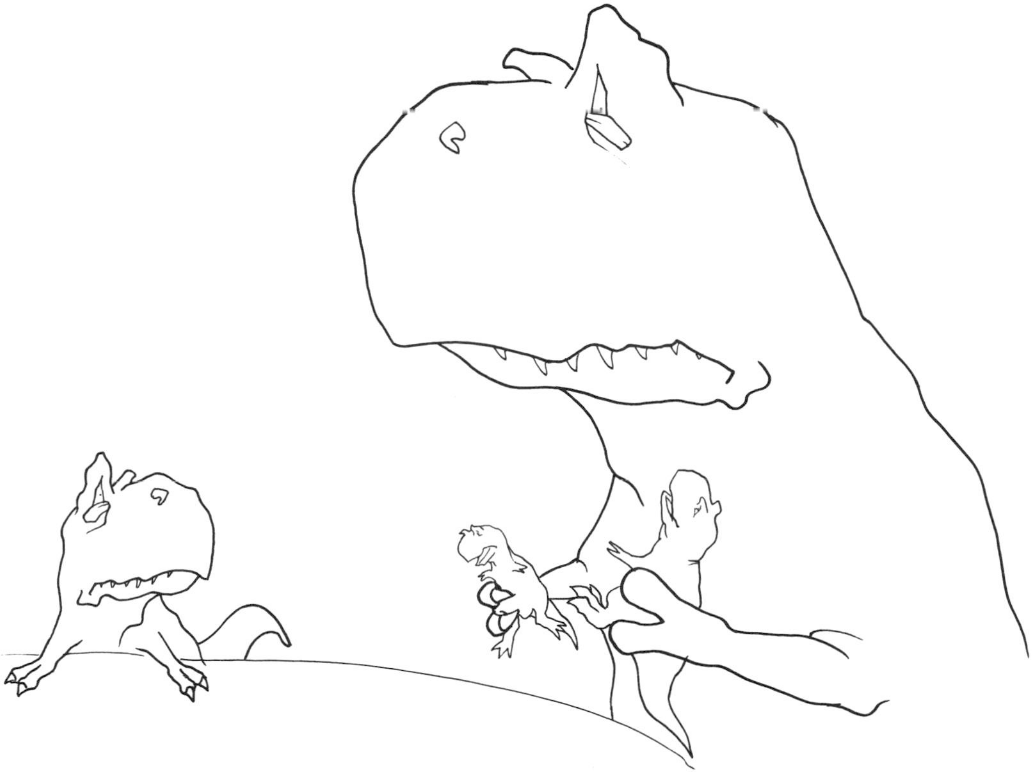

T-Rex trying to explain where wee-rexes come from . . .

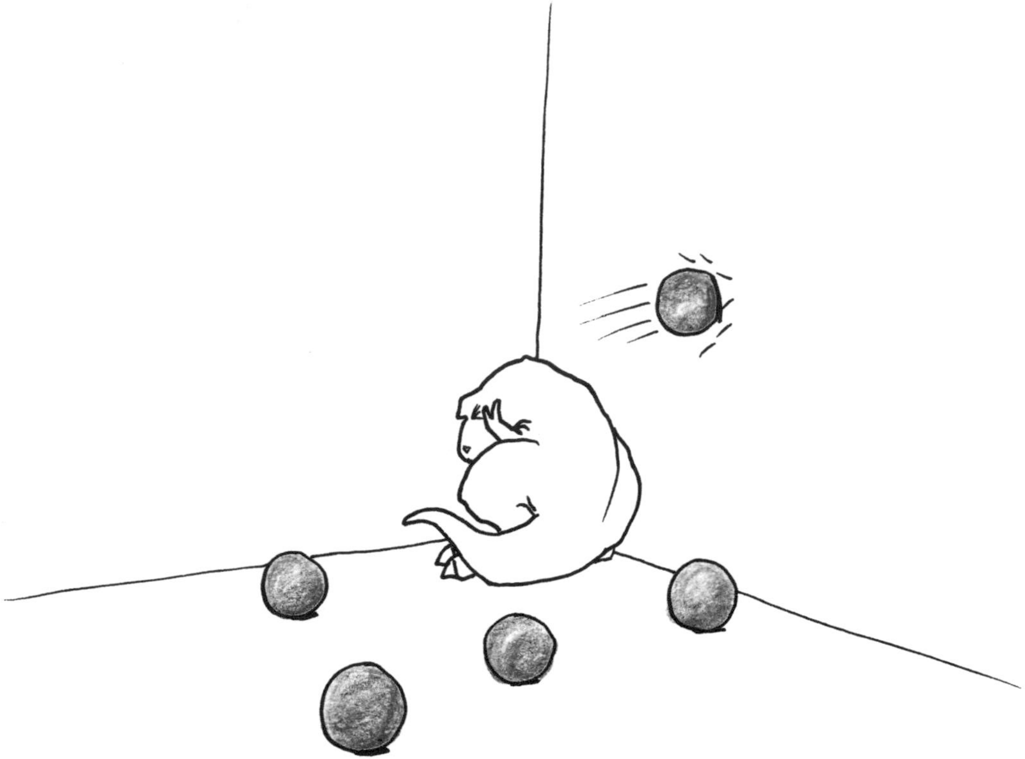

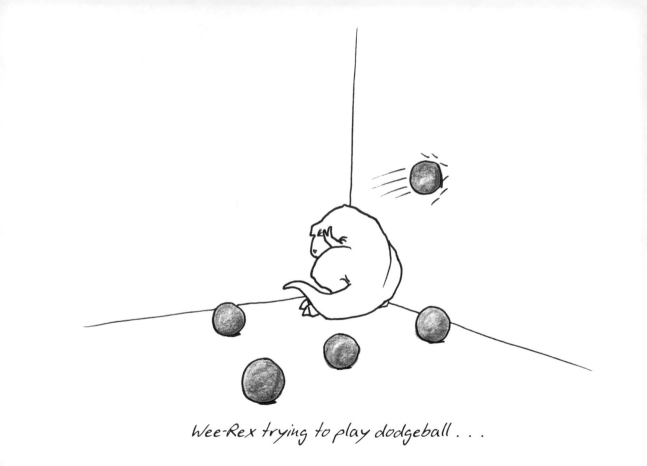

Wee-Rex trying to play dodgeball . . .

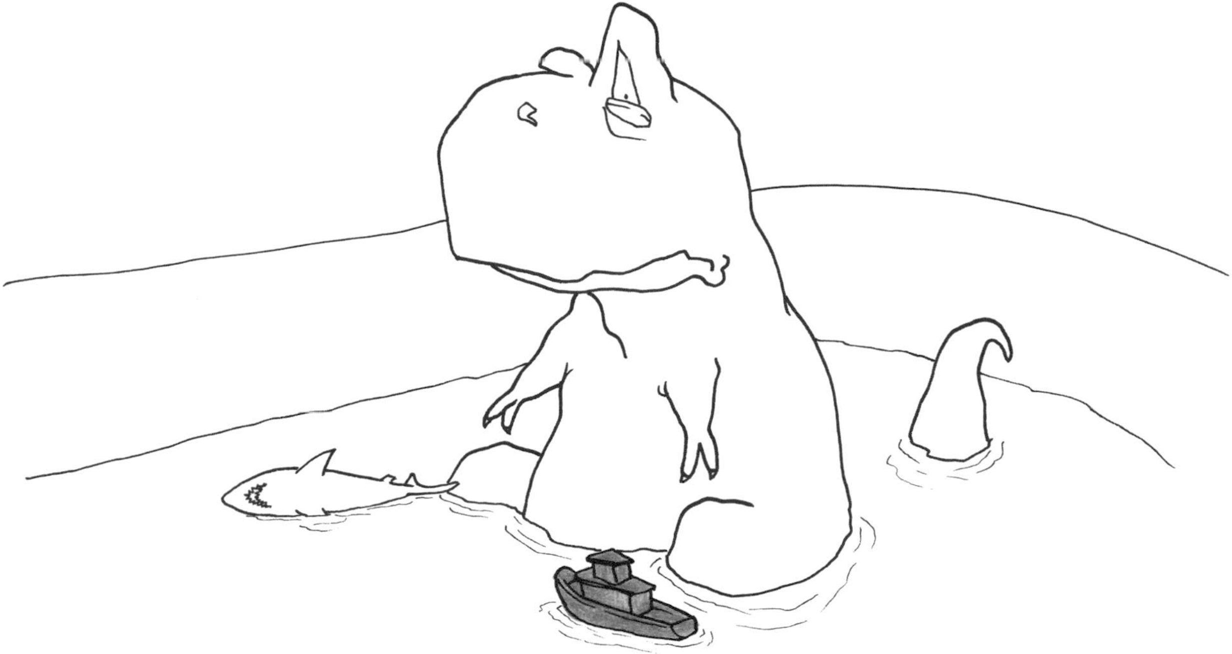

Wee-Rex trying to play with his toys in the bath . . .

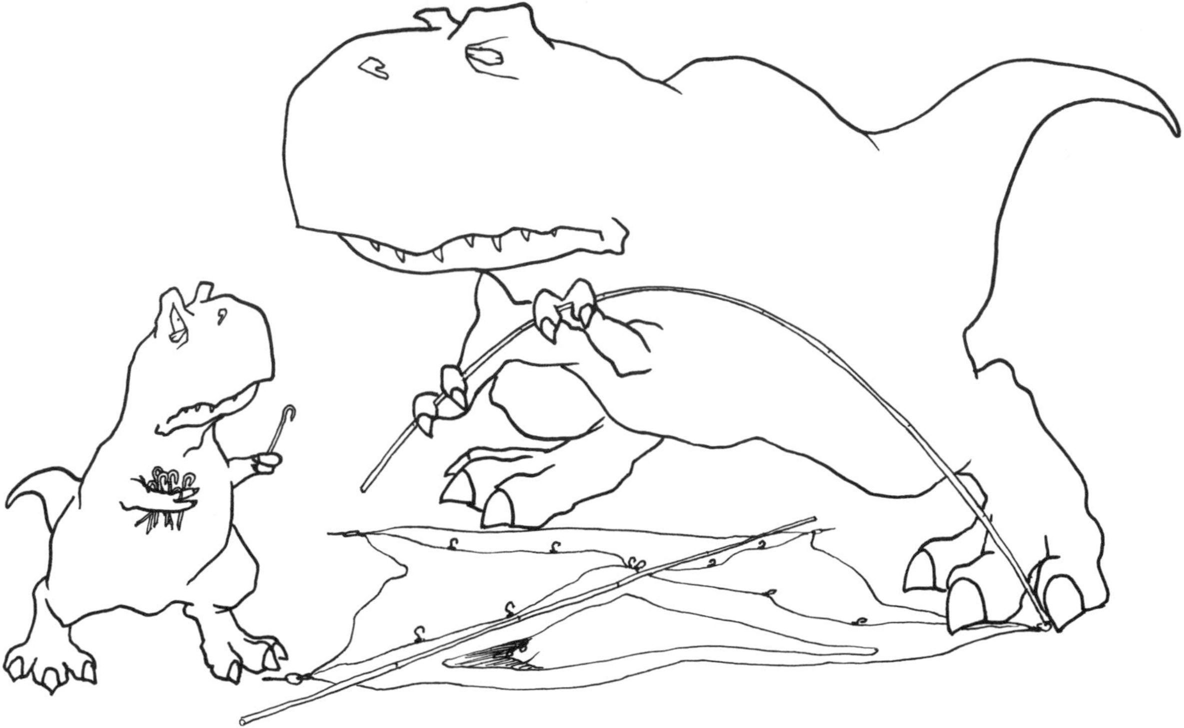

T-Rex and Wee-Rex trying to pitch a tent . . .

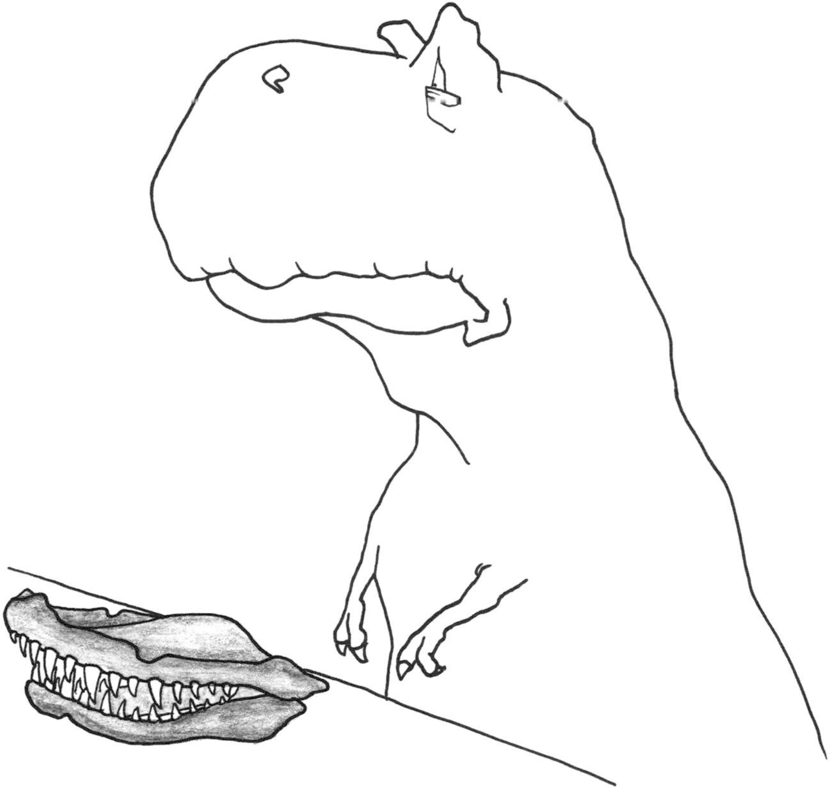

T-Rex trying to put on his dentures . . .

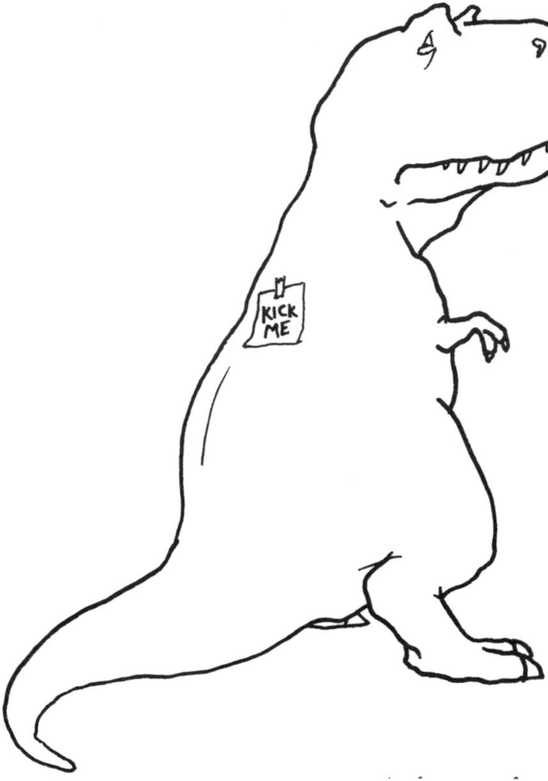
KICK ME

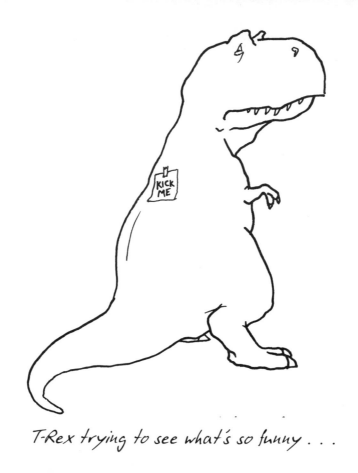

T-Rex trying to see what's so funny . . .

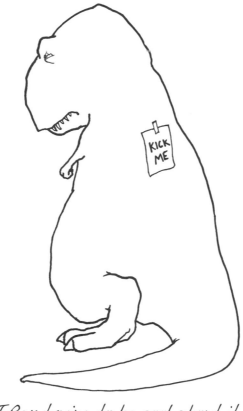

T-Rex trying to be cool about it . . .

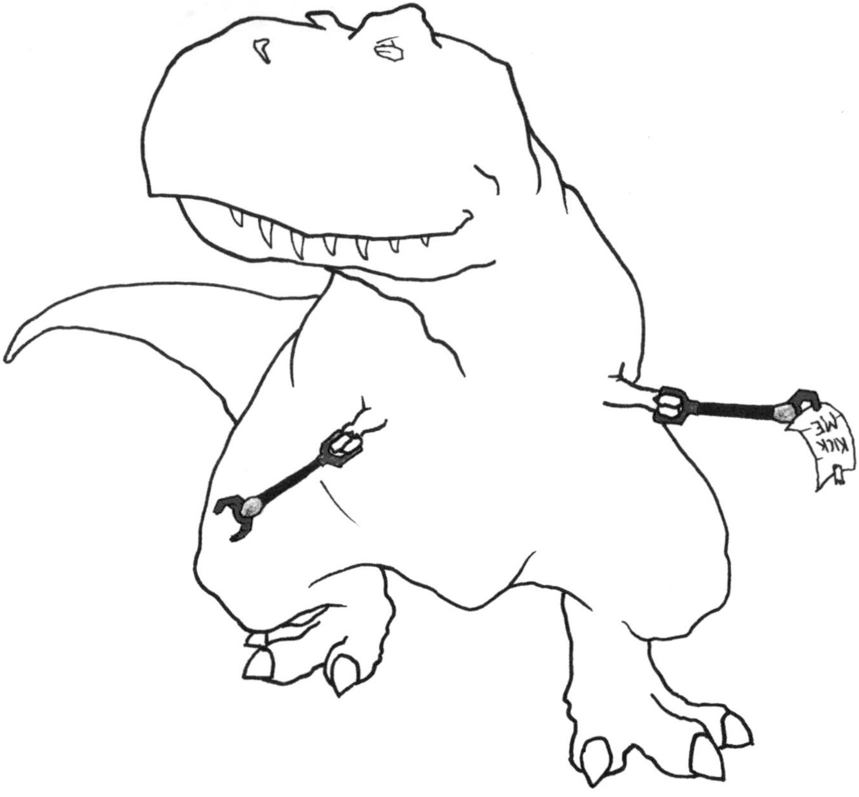
KICK ME

T-Rex trying to preserve his dignity . . .